8 THE GAME IS ON

8 THE GAME IS ON

SWAPNIL KHAMKAR

Srishti
PUBLISHERS & DISTRIBUTORS

SRISHTI PUBLISHERS & DISTRIBUTORS
Registered Office: N-16, C.R. Park
New Delhi – 110 019
Corporate Office: 212A, Peacock Lane
Shahpur Jat, New Delhi – 110 049
editorial@srishtipublishers.com

First published by
Srishti Publishers & Distributors in 2018

Dedicated to
my mom and dad, and to the time that surrounded me
from all the directions to make me fall.

'Sab kuch tabah ho sakta hai,
Par jigar nahi...'

A note from the author

All artwork, monuments and historic references mentioned in this novel are real.

The Pilgrim Ship incident related to Vasco da Gama mentioned in this novel is real.

On 15 March 2016, the Omani Government stated that they discovered a ship named *Esmeralda*, which belonged to Vasco da Gama.

Esmeralda had sunk in the Arabian Sea in the year 1503.

The artefacts mentioned in this novel are real.

The film, *Urumi*, released in 2011, was based on the failed attempt to kill Vasco da Gama.

Acknowledgements

Firstly, I would like to thank my entire family for supporting me and believing in me. Thanks to my dad Sanjay Khamkar, mom Pratibha Khamkar, and brother Pushpak Khamkar. Thanks to my grandparents, Harishchandra and Taramati Khamkar, for their constant support.

Special thanks to my cousin, Snehal. I must say, without your belief in me, I wouldn't have been able to write this book. Thanks to my cousins, Shoan, Manav, Neha, Parag, Darshana, Ritika, Pratik and Rohan, for inspiring me and encouraging me to write.

And here are my friends, Gaurav Pawar, Devendra Palve, Yogesh Payal, Abhishek Deshpande, Mohak, Sadik, Siddharth, Sanket, Gautam, Ashok, Sumedh, Aditya, Sudarshan, Swapnil and Balaji. Thank you everyone for always keeping me motivated and enthusiastic.

Thanks to my teachers, Desle sir and Shelke sir.

Thanks to the entire team of Srishti, for believing in me and guiding me in the entire publishing procedure.

Last but not the least, thanks to the person who is no more in my life. I would only say that I lost you but I found myself.

Prologue

Chennai, India

The sky was dark. There wasn't a single twinkling star. Not a single person had the guts to look up at the open sky. The rain had made its way down. The pain was so immense that someone had to cry. The clouds took it upon themselves and cried heavily. The water was continuously pouring over the streets, washing away all the mud and dirt on the road, over the vehicles and houses.

The street had large bungalows. Out of them, the largest was that of a film director. With the huge success of his last film, he was ready to start his work on another blockbuster. His house was huge, quite, spacious and luxurious. The parking would always be full with luxurious cars. He enjoyed all the top-most facilities in his life. His wife was a homemaker and they had no children.

The director was above forty years and his wife a few years younger. But the almighty had not blessed them with a child. They always thought of adopting a child, but their busy schedules didn't allow them to get down to it.

That night, the house was locked. All the workers and security guards were on a holiday. All the cars were in the parking lot and all the lights were off, except the street light. The area was silent and the streets were empty. The house turned into a ghost house that night. The body of the director was found hanging in his bedroom. A chair had been thrown aside. The rope was tied to the ceiling fan. The room was dark and lightning flashed a shadow of the hanging body.

The director, Akash Gupta had been an alcoholic and chain smoker. He was talented in his work, but could never work without taking a sip of some costly liquor. He made blockbuster films back to back and was counted as one of the best directors in south India.

His friend, Shivam Saran, informed the police at 2:30 a.m. Shivam too was a film director. The police reached the house at 3:15 a.m. and sealed the house. The only person present at the spot apart from the police was Shivam.

It time was about 6 a.m. The phone was ringing and disturbing Neel's sleep. Neel managed to look at the phone's screen and then kept it aside. The phone rang again. Neel tried hard to ignore it, but couldn't.

'What is it Jay? Why are you so annoying?' Neel screamed on the phone.

'The police needs you Neel. There was an incident last night,' said Jay.

'I don't want to help anyone. And I have resigned, so please let me sleep,' Neel said with his eyes closed.

'But the department has not accepted your resignation,' Jay commented.

'I don't care! If the department is taking my family away from me, then I am not interested in entertaining them.'

'Neel, this is a high profile case. The film director Akash Gupta has committed suicide.'

'What? Why?' Neel was wide awake now.

'Reason unknown. We need you Neel. I will text you the address.'

'Fine,' Neel said and ended the call.

Neel got up from his bed yawning. His half-closed eyes fell on the portrait hung up right in front on the wall.

Why have you gone away, my beautiful wife? When will you learn the truth?

Neel stared at the portrait with tears in his eyes. He then managed to walk up to the washbasin. He switched on the light and saw his tired face in the mirror. There was a dark stubble on his cheeks. The eyes were tired and his face was dull.

I need my wife to fix my face!

After having a shower, Neel searched for a decent shirt in his wardrobe. His eyes fell on a red shirt. He took out the shirt and touched the stain on the collar.

It still has not gone. Like a stain on my life!

He put the shirt back into the wardrobe and randomly picked up a white shirt and wore it. He left the house, took out his sedan and headed towards the address. Then he dialled Jay's number.

'Where are you Jay? Come with me. I am coming to pick you up,' Neel said and ended the call without listening to what Jay had to say.

He picked up Jay and they headed towards Akash Gupta's house.

'What have you done to yourself, Neel? Why can't you come to terms with it? I know it was not your fault, but why are you blaming the police department for it? What is their role in your personal matter?' Jay asked Neel.

'It has all happened because of the department. I don't want to talk about it.'

'Has Avantika called?' Jay asked, and as soon as he spoke out the name, Neel glared at him.

'I mean, is her decision final?' asked Jay.

'What is left now? She has resigned from the department. She has sent me the divorce papers. What is left to make it more certain?' asked Neel.

'But neither of your resignation letters has been accepted. Not even hers,' explained Jay.

'I don't care! And if you speak any further, then I will forget that you are my friend,' Neel said pointing to his gun.

Jay had no option but to keep silent. After a short drive, they reached their destination. Neel parked his sedan outside the house, keeping a distance between them. He meticulously glanced at the road and the footpath. He took out his cell phone and clicked two pictures, one of the footpath where the entry gate was, and another of the road. He then took out his pocket-sized notepad and noted down something.

Jay was giving Neel a strange look. Neel signalled Jay to move into the house. They both went inside the house and Neel rolled his eyes in all directions. He checked the doors and windows. Then he checked the furniture. Then they moved into the bedroom. The body was still hanging from the fan. As Neel had demanded, no one had entered the bedroom before him. He went close to the body and saw the shoes. The shoes had mud on it. Mud stains were also present on the trousers. The clothes were dry and cold. Neel ordered his police companions to take the body down.

They untied the rope and lay the body down on the floor. Neel examined the neck and it had a clear visible dark-red line over it. The rope was very strong and had no effect of the weight it had been carrying. The nails had mud on it. The shirt was clean.

'Who informed you about the suicide?' Neel asked Jay.

'It was director Shivam Saran,' Jay said and signalled the other police officer to call him. The other police officer called the director Shivam Saran inside the room. He entered with a red face. It was evident that he had been crying.

'When did you come to know about it?' Neel asked.

'When I came to Akash's house at night, I saw the house was in darkness. There was no light. The streetlight was on. The main door was open. So I went inside to check. And when I entered his bedroom, I saw his body hanging,' Shivam said in a low voice.

'At what time did you see the body?' asked Neel.

'It must have been around 2:15 to 2:20 in the morning,' said Shivam.

'And what were you doing at his house at that time? It is an odd time to visit someone,' said Neel.

'Yes, but the life of a film director is very different from normal people. I had come to give him the manuscript of his next movie. We both were working on a script and Akash had been waiting or the complete manuscript for a long time. He demanded that it be handed over to him whenever it was ready. So I went to his house,' explained Shivam.

'Did Akash know you were coming? When did you last speak with him?'

'No, he didn't know. I wanted to give him a surprise. When I got a call from the screenplay writer that the manuscript was ready, I immediately picked it up from his office at 1:00 a.m. and headed towards Akash's home. I spoke to him in the evening at about 8:30 p.m. for the last time.'

'How far is this screenplay writer's office from here? And what is his name?'

'It's about fifteen kilometres away. His name is Shankar Deo.'

'It took one hour for you to drive from his office till here? One hour to cover only fifteen kilometres? Isn't that strange?'

'No, actually I took the manuscript from his office and went home before coming here.'

'How far is your home from here?'

'I think it's about five kilometres away.'

'Did anyone see you when you went home after taking the manuscript?'

'Yes, my wife was at home. She even shouted at me for going to visit Akash so late.'

'Fine. You will have to come to the police station whenever we call you,' Neel said and signalled to him to leave.

'Where is Akash's wife? Why is she not here?' Neel asked Jay.

'She's out of town, at her mother's place. She will be reaching here in the afternoon,' said Jay.

'What do you think? Is it a suicide or a murder?' Jay asked as they sat in the car.

'Murder,' said Neel reversing the car.

'Yes, I think so as well.'

'Yesterday night it was raining heavily. The entrance has ruts made by the wheels indicating entering and leaving multiple times. But according to Shivam, he was here from 2 a.m. and did not leave the house after that. He is not telling us the truth. Akash's shoes have the same mud on them. His nails have mud in them, his trousers have that mud stains, which mean he had been walking in the mud. But there is no such area nearby. And all the cars are clean at home. Only one car has mud stains on its tyres and that car belongs to Shivam. Even though it was pouring, the rain could not wash away the mud. That means the car was in a large muddy area or maybe stuck in the mud. A slight red mark on the left side of Akash's face indicates that he was hit or was slapped,' explained Neel.

'Oh! Yes, you are right,' Jay said and paused.

'I want to meet the screenwriter Shankar Deo.'

'I will call him to the police station.'

'No, not there! We will go to his office.'

'Fine,' Jay said and started searching for his office address on the GPS.

When they reached Shankar's office, he was in his cabin working on the laptop. Jay and Neel went inside his cabin.

Neel asked point-blank, 'Did you murder Akash Gupta?'

'W... What? What are you saying! Who are you?' stuttered Shankar in surprise.

'The police!' said Jay.

'He was my friend. Why would I murder him?' said Shankar in fear.

'What do you know about Akash's murder?' asked Neel.

'Shivam told me about the suicide. I was shocked. He was my dear friend. We were working on a script and I had never expected he would commit suicide,' said Shankar.

'When did Shivam call you?' asked Neel.

'Around 2:30 in the morning.'

'Where were you when he called you?' asked Neel.

'In my office. I was working on a script,' said Shankar.

'Don't you sleep?' asked Jay.

'When did you last meet Akash?' asked Neel.

'Yesterday, in my office. Shivam and Akash had come to check the script of their film.'

'Did you notice anything strange? Any strange behaviour?' asked Neel.

'Yes, he was sweating a lot! He is always normal. But yesterday, he seemed different. He did not even smoke. Usually he always has a cigar in his hand,' said Shankar.

'Does your office have CCTV camera?' asked Neel.

'Yes, but they are switched off,' said Shankar.

'Did anyone see the three of you yesterday in your office?' asked Neel.

'No! Usually there is no one else in my office.'

'You are a well-known screenwriter. And there is no one at your office? Not even security. If I stab you, no one would ever know,' said Jay.

'This office is private and no one knows about my office.'

'Fine, so there is no proof that you three met yesterday,' Neel said.

'Why would I lie?' asked Shankar.

'I don't know,' Neel said and got up to leave.

'He doesn't know!' Jay said as they left the office.

Neel and Jay sat in the car and Neel asked, 'Where is Akash's wife? Why is she not here?'

'I will find out more and tell you,' Jay said.

'I want to know and interrogate her as early as possible.'

'What do you think of Shankar?'

'Can't say! According to his expression, he looked frightened. Is the fear due to the suicide or murder? And why is he so early at the office? It is 9:30. If he was working the previous night till say 3 o'clock, then how did he wake up so early? His eyes looked too active and had no sign of soreness. It seems that he knew the police would come to his office for interrogation. And that is why he is at the office so early,' explained Neel.

'Well, you are clever! But you missed one thing.'

'What?'

'Shankar said he was Akash's friend. If the three were working on the same film, they must have been working closely. Then why is he here? Why did he not go to see his friend? Is this friendship?' questioned Jay.

'Yes, but this is common sense. I know this already.'

'What do you think of his wife? Do you think she is involved in this murder?'

'So you have deduced that it is a murder?'

'Maybe! Can't say with certainty.'

'How much money does Akash have in banks and other assets?'

'I don't know the exact figure, but it is around five million.'

'And who would get the money after him?'

'There is an NGO in Chennai. He donates money to them.'

'What work does the NGO do?'

'Takes care of handicapped kids. There is a school.'

'Who owns the school?'

'Akash.'

'Is there nothing that goes to his wife?'

'Only their house.'

'What is the cost of the house?'

'Around fifty million.'

'Well then we will have to talk to his wife. By the way, where is Akash's phone?'

'It's missing. It was last traced in his house, but it is not there.'

'At what time was it last traced?'

'Around 11:30, it was switched off. That time the phone was at home. And his last call was at about 11 p.m. He spoke to his wife.'

'How did you know it was his wife's number?'

'We have all the numbers, Neel. We are not idiots, though I know you think we are.'

'Then, did you talk to his wife?'

'Yes, she was totally shocked. And she said Akash seemed scared when she spoke to him. She was crying hysterically when we spoke to her. I think she is innocent.'

'The truth is not based on our perspectives.'

'Yes, I am an idiot!'

'Akash told me to visit my parents. When I was leaving, he was normal. But two days earlier, he seemed worried. I asked him, but he just changed the topic,' said Janvi Gupta, Akash's wife.

'What was he worried about? Was he involved in any disputes or any other thing that would lead him to take such an extreme step?' asked Neel.

'No, never! He was kind-hearted and did not face any such thing that would provoke him to do this. I just can't believe he is no more. I cannot accept that he has committed suicide,' said Janvi, crying.

'So you think it is a murder?' asked Neel.

'But why would anyone murder him?'

'What did he say to you when he last spoke? Did he drop a hint?'

'No, he just asked me to take care. He said he loves me and nothing more. It was a normal conversation and he always used the same words while speaking to me. But he seemed a bit scared yesterday. His voice was hardly audible and he spoke fast.'

'When did you leave him?'

'I went to my parents' house three days ago. He forced me to go. He said that I hadn't visited my parents for many days. I didn't suspect anything as he was always kind to me and my parents.'

'Fine, we will investigate and find the actual reason behind the death. Thank you for your co-operation,' said Neel.

Neel and Jay left Akash's house. Neel asked Jay about the worker and the security guard.

'They were sent off. Akash told them that he needed to be alone and therefore he asked them to go for a holiday,' said Jay.

'Where are they from?'

'A small village near Chennai. They said that Akash was frustrated that day. They know nothing else.'

'I think we should interrogate Shivam.'

'Yes, but he will never tell us the truth. And we have no warrant to arrest him and extract the truth from him.'

Suddenly, Neel's phone rang. Neel saw the screen and said, 'It's Raghu.'

'Good afternoon sir!' Neel greeted.

'Neel, come to my office immediately,' said Raghu Iyer, the Additional Superintendent of Police and Neel's mentor. Neel had immense respect for him.

'Yes sir. I will be there,' Neel said and the call ended.

'Raghu wants us in his office,' Neel told Jay.

'Well then, let's go!'

When Neel and Jay entered Raghu's cabin, he was reading some file. As soon as he saw Neel and Jay, he kept the file aside and told them to have a seat.

'Neel, you have an assignment,' said Raghu.

'We are currently investigating Akash Gupta's case,' said Neel.

'Leave that case! We have other officers to look after that,' said Raghu. Raghu got up from his seat, switched off the lights and put on the projector.

'Look at these pictures, Neel. There is a shipwreck found in Oman. The ship sank in 1503. It was a Portuguese carrack that belonged to Vasco da Gama,' said Raghu.

'Oh! It is a great discovery,' said Neel.

'No, there has been an incident. The artefacts found in the ship have been stolen. The Intelligence Bureau says that they were stolen by a group of Indians.'

'Oh! But how did it happen?'

'When the artefacts were discovered and taken to the laboratory for testing, some people looted the truck. They had only two security guards. The thieves had guns. Thank god, no one was killed. They sprayed some kind of liquid which put the security guards off to sleep.'

'Strange thing! But why would anyone steal the artefacts?'

'That is your job to find out. You have to go to Oman tomorrow itself. Take the report and find out what is wrong,' said Raghu and handed over a file to Neel.

'Am I going alone?'

'No, Jay will accompany you. The Oman police will be working with you as well.'

Jay was shocked to hear his name. It was his first assignment out of India. After taking the necessary documents and the tickets, Jay and Neel left the office.

'Neel, I am nervous! I haven't worked on any assignment out of India,' said Jay sitting in the car.

'Don't be nervous! It is not going to be exciting,' replied Neel.

'When is the flight?'

'Tomorrow evening at 7:30 p.m. Air India flight no. 907.'

'But where are we going in Oman?'

'To the capital of Oman, Muscat.'

Neel was getting ready for his departure. He packed his bag and went for a shower. After the refreshing shower, he wore a brand new black shirt and black formal trousers. He took out his black blazer, which Avantika had gifted to him on his previous birthday. It reminded him of Avantika. He wore the blazer and sat on the bed, brooding over the past. He remembered the day when she threw the cup of coffee on his shirt. He was silent. She was crying.

I will miss you, my dear wife!

After a while, he got up and wore his shoes. He came out of the bedroom with his bag. The house felt too empty without her. He locked the house and went out of the gate. Jay was waiting for him in the taxi. Jay saw Neel in the formal clothes and cleared his throat.

'You look handsome!' Jay commented.

'I didn't ask you for an opinion,' Neel replied.

'Does Avantika know you are going?'

'Shut up!'

'Fine, but when can I speak? And when can she know the truth? Why can't you just tell her that you love her and it is all a misunderstanding?'

'She is not in the state to listen to me. And I have nothing to prove to her. She knows that I love her. And when the time will be right, I will speak to her.'

'As you wish,' said Jay.

Neel and Jay reached the Chennai International Airport. The building was shining in the evening light. Most of the part of the mega-structure was recently constructed. They went for the departures terminal.

After having their seats, Jay asked, 'Are you ready?

'What for?'

'The trip.'

'It is not a trip. Don't think of it as a trip.'

Four hours later, the plane landed at the Muscat International Airport. The time was about 10 p.m. The time in Oman is an hour and a half behind IST. Neel and Jay went out of the airport and took a cab. Neel told the taxi driver the address of the hotel and they were soon on their way.

After reaching the hotel, Neel and Jay checked in into their respective suites. Settling down a bit, they went down for dinner. Jay was relaxed and was enjoying the food and the stay in the hotel. He was excited about his assignment now.

The next morning, Jay and Neel went to the Indian Embassy located in an area called Ruwi in Muscat. Neel went inside the building to meet the Indian Ambassador, Rahul Mishra. They went into his cabin and Rahul greeted him.

Neel showed the file to Rahul and requested that he be allowed to visit the site with the Oman police. Rahul saw the file and said, 'I will talk to the authorities and you will be able to visit the place tomorrow. The Oman police have already been informed about your arrival. Enjoy your stay in Oman.'

'Thank you for your assistance,' said Neel.

'You can leave your address here. We will give your address to the respective officers and they will be able to meet you there.'

'Yes, of course!' Neel said and gave him the address.

Rahul arranged a car for Neel and Jay so that they would be able to move around in the city. They went back to the hotel and Neel went into his suite. He heard a knock on the door after a while. It was Jay.

'The Oman officials are here to meet you,' said Jay.

'Send them in,' said Neel.

Two police officers entered the room. One of them said, 'Welcome sir, I hope you like your stay in Oman.' Neel nodded and gestured to them to have a seat.

'I am glad you can speak English,' said Neel.

'Yes, of course! It's our secondary language, but we have no problem in communicating,' said the officer.

'So what is the report on the shipwreck?' asked Neel.

'The shipwreck was discovered in the second week of March near the Al-Hallaniyah Island. Then the artefacts were studied and taken to the laboratory. But on the way, a group of people looted the truck. Two officers were injured and we have no information after that,' said the officer.

'But why were they stolen? Any specific reason? Or any specific history?'

'The artefacts were discovered from the ship *Esmeralda*, which was the ship commanded by Vasco da Gama's maternal uncles, Bras Sodre and Vicente Sodre. The ship played an important part in Da Gama's second voyage to India. The ship sank in 1503. Out of five carrack ships, the two ships namely *Esmeralda* and *Sao Pedro* sank near the south coast of Oman. They were found approximately forty-five kilometres off the southern coast of Oman.'

'But what has the thief to do with the artefacts? Do they have any specific history? And what about an Indian playing a role in this scenario?'

'The two policemen, who guarded the truck, said that the thieves spoke in Hindi and English. The artefacts have no specific history. The secret agency of Oman thinks that the artefacts were stolen by Indian people. As Vasco da Gama has a history with India, the ship and the artefacts may co-relate to some of Da Gama's stay in India.'

'Fine, but we will have proof only when I visit the site and study the other artefacts,' commented Neel.

'Yes sir, we will visit the site tomorrow. You will be able to take a look at the other artefacts and deduce a conclusion,' replied the officer.

'Where have the other artefacts been kept?'

'In a laboratory in Muscat. The security has been increased due to the incident. The main artefacts such as coins and other major discoveries have been stolen. It is confirmed that the thieves stole only the main articles and not the others. It proves that it has something to do with the history of the articles and the ship,' said the officer.

'Fine, I will see to it that it is investigated properly,' said Neel.

After the officials left, Neel and Jay went for lunch. Grabbing Neel's attention, Jay asked, 'Can we go out to explore the city?'

Neel heard him, but remained silent.

'We have a car now and a driver too who can speak English,' said Jay. 'We have to visit the lab tomorrow. We have an evening free.'

'Fine, nice idea,' said Neel.

Jay broke out into an enthusiastic laugh surprised to hear Neel's words.

'Are you really ready? Or you are just trying to fool me?'

'Come before I change my mind,' said Neel and got up from the chair. 'Come to my room after paying the bill.'

Jay got up immediately, kept the amount on the table and told the waiter to take away the bill. He went to his suite and got ready. Then he went and knocked on Neel's room. Neel opened the door and Jay was surprised to see Neel in jeans and a t-shirt.

'We are at the Seeb International Hotel. Ruwi is twenty kilometres from here. First, we will visit the Royal Opera House Muscat and then go to Ruwi. Then we will go to the Muttrah Corniche,' said Neel.

'I don't know any of the places, but it sounds good!'

Then Neel and Jay went to the parking of the hotel. The car and the driver were waiting for them. Neel had already informed the driver about the visit. The beautiful city and the well-constructed buildings attracted their eyes. The clean roads and the fresh air made Jay look everywhere his eyes reached. The sky was clear blue and the sunshine bright. The essence of Arabian construction was clearly seen in every single building. The modern city was interspersed by history with its domes and towers.

After the half-hour drive, Neel and Jay reached the Royal Opera House. The brightly shining white multi buildings represent the art and culture of Oman. The Islamic and Italian architecture and the large building bound in awe anyone who sees it for the very first time.

Neel and Jay entered the building and were stunned to see the infrastructure. The greenery in front of the building, the open blue sky on top of the building and the pure white man-made beauty rejuvenated their hearts.

'That is what we call the creation of an art lover,' said Jay. 'The Sultan is an art and music lover.'

Neel nodded and said, 'But we have many historical and beautiful monuments in India as well.'

After a short visit to the Opera House, Neel and Jay left for Corniche located in Muttrah. It was located on the banks of the Arabian Sea. The place is famous for its food and it's a great place to walk around. The coastline road is an example of the scenic beauty of the city.

When they reached the place and started walking down the street alongside of the coast, Jay said, 'It is so similar to the Mumbai coastline. Feels like we are in Mumbai.'

Neel said nothing and just looked at the waves of the sea. After seeing Neel's expression, Jay understood that Neel was missing Avantika.

'Missing someone?' asked Jay.

'Why would I miss anyone?' answered Neel.

'I mean Avantika,' said Jay and patted on Neel's shoulder. It was the very first brave act by Jay. He knew Neel was missing Avantika. He was trying to console Neel, but it didn't affect Neel in any manner.

'Can't you just stay out of that matter? Why are you ruining my trip?'

'I am sorry. I didn't mean to hurt you,' said Jay. 'Leave it! Look at the ship near the coast. It's so big!'

Neel was silent. He knew Jay was his one true friend. He knew Jay was right, but he avoided the topic.

After a walk, they ended up at one of the innumerable food stalls. They tasted many of the dishes and enjoyed them immensely.

Later, they went to the base of the Muttrah Fort. The fort was glowing in the darkness. The lights brought out the magnificence of the fort as Jay clicked a few pictures. Standing at the base of the fort, one can see the entire coastline and the beautiful envelope of lights over the coastline. Night had fallen to brighten and lighten the city and to make it look even more radiant.

Jay and Neel finally tore away from the place when they realized that they had to go back to their hotel. They had to work on an important assignment the next day. Jay wanted to stay a little longer, but he followed Neel as he walked towards their car.

They reached the hotel and went into their respective suites. Neel took out his cell phone, opened the gallery and looked at a photo. Neel and Avantika looked beautiful together. Her glowing white skin, her natural black long hair partially on Neel's shoulder, her romantic eyes and their eternal love. The photo represented it all.

They both were very happy that day. Neel had proposed to her unexpectedly. She was shocked when Neel went down on his knees and handed a red rose to her in a coffee shop. All the other people had applauded. Avantika, without any hesitation, had said yes. Neel had taken her in his arms and had whispered in her ears, 'I love you Avantika. Thank you.'

'I love you too Neel,' she had said.

Neel recalled the scene and a smile appeared on his face. He kept the phone aside and closed his eyes.

The next morning, Neel got up and glanced out of his room's window. The traffic was flowing and the city was back to work. The tall buildings shone in the sunshine and reflected the vast blue sky.

After getting ready, Neel and Jay contacted the Indian Embassy. The two officers in black suits were already waiting for Neel and Jay at the waiting area of the hotel. As soon as Neel and Jay came down from their suites, the two officers greeted them and told them that they were there to take them to the lab.

Neel and Jay went with them and sat in the car. The driver took them to the archeological lab. The lab was spacious and luxurious and housed many artefacts. Neel and Jay went into the cabin of the officer in-charge. He took them to the highly secured area where the artefacts from the ship were kept. The cameras and the fingerprint scanner guarded the entrance of the room. An armed officer was standing outside the lab.

The three of them entered the room and the in-charge showed them the artefacts.

'Only eight artefacts are missing from the 2000 articles,' said the officer.

'Can I get the list of articles found and articles missing,' asked Neel.

'Yes, of course! Here is the list,' the officer said as the papers were in his hand. He gave them to Neel.

Neel scanned the list of the missing items.

'The artefacts missing are rare and historical. The eight artefacts are – a bell dated the year 1498, a bronze Arquebus barrel; a 'VS' mark cannon ball, a copper alloy disc, a large block sheave, a Manuel cruzado coin, a gold cruzado coin, and white agate and carnelian beads,' said the officer.

'The artefacts have no connection with each other. Why would anyone steal a bell, a disc and beads?' Neel said to himself.

'Do you know anything about these articles? The history or any other information on these articles? Why have these items been stolen?' asked Neel.

'No, we don't have any information about these items,' replied the officer.

'Was there any form of communication from the thieves? Any phone call or demand or any mail or any letter?' asked Neel.

'No, nothing yet!' replied the officer. 'That is the main issue. We do not understand the reason behind this robbery.'

'Have you contacted the Portuguese?'

'No! The authority doesn't feel it's right to contact them until we find out the reason behind this robbery.'

'Fine! Can you give me the photographs of the stolen items?' asked Neel.

'Sure! But we insist you to handle the matter with care and not publicize the issue and the photos. As there is a history connected to the artefacts, it is a sensitive issue,' said the officer.

'Don't worry! I will not forget the protocol,' said Neel. He went on to look at the other artefacts. Some of the gold and silver coins had been kept in the room. After lying in water for five hundred years, the coins were still shining and the embedded insignia was still clearly visible on the coins.

Some copper alloy breech chambers had also been laid out for analysis. They had gathered a little rust on them and were representative of the culture and lifestyle of the sailors and the people living five hundred years ago.

There were ceramic articles, pots and the like as well. Neel looked at each one carefully. He knew he had to study those articles to find the missing ones.

After having a look at the articles, the three of them went into the office. Neel called Raghu from the office.

'Sir, we have found that eight artefacts are missing from the discovery,' said Neel over the phone.

'Any specific reason behind the robbery? Do the articles represent anything? Or any specific person or place?' asked Raghu.

'No sir, we don't have any information concerning that yet.'

'Any connection with history? Any contact with the Portuguese?'

'No sir.'

'Fine, you leave for Lisbon tonight. I have made the arrangements. You both go and talk with the Portuguese authorities and let me know about it.'

'Sir, but I don't think the Portuguese have any information regarding this case,' said Neel.

'But it's our duty to go and talk with them. Or the Omani and the Portuguese will think we are responsible for the theft.'

'Fine, no problem,' said Neel and ended the call.

After their meeting, Neel and Jay came out of the office. They sat in the car and headed back to the hotel.

'What did he say?' asked Jay.

'Time to fly again! He has asked us to go to Portugal and find out more about this case,' said Neel.

'Wow! Feels like an adventure,' Jay said gleefully.

After having lunch, Neel went into his suite to pack his bag. He went close to the window and glanced at the road. He saw a couple, walking hand in hand enjoying each other's presence. It reminded Neel of his time when he and Avantika enjoyed walking together at a beach in Chennai.

She had been happy that day. Neel and Avantika had decided to get married and they were having a wonderful time at the beach. Neel remembered how she splashed water over him. Neel too, did not miss the chance and had caught her in his arms.

'So you want to make me wet?' said Neel and grabbed her.

She laughed and said, 'Yes. You look more handsome when you are wet.'

'But this is not the right place. We can do this at home,' said Neel as she was trying to land a kiss on his cheeks.

'Then let's go home,' she said and hugged Neel.

They immediately went and sat in the car. The sun was setting and night was about to fall. Neel and Avantika were in a romantic mood and they did not leave the opportunity to kiss each other.

As soon as their lips touched, Neel came back into his senses. He took his bag and went to the reception of the hotel. Jay was paying the bill and completing the formalities. Neel went and put his bag in the car. Jay joined him after a while and they left for the Muscat International Airport.

'How much time do we need to get to Lisbon?' asked Jay.

'Twelve hours,' answered Neel.

'So long! What will we do in the flight?'

'Sleep!'

'Muscat is three hours ahead of Lisbon. We will have to adjust to the timings again,' Jay almost complained.

'Yes, after all, the Indian government has made all the arrangements for our stay in Lisbon. We don't have any choice,' Neel was to the point, like always.

Jay made a face which reflected confusion, and Neel continued, 'You are lucky enough to catch two international cities in one trip!'

'Yes, it's your grace! Thanks for choosing me as your coordinator,' Jay said sarcastically.

'I didn't choose you. It is the mistake of the department.'

'Oh, it's not a mistake! Have I disturbed you? Have I ruined your trip and your assignment? I have paid all the bills and all the fares!'

'It is the government who has paid, so stop taking credit!'

'Even though it is the government's money, one should know where to spend and where not,' Jay retorted.

'Fine! Stop arguing! I will have to bear you for the next fourteen hours anyway.'

'It's twelve!'

'Two at the airport!'

Neel and Jay reached the airport and went to the departures section. Jay went out to grab some snacks. Neel was busy thinking about the missing artefacts.

'The canon ball, the alloy disc, the beads, the bell, and the sheave. What is the use of these articles?' he asked himself. He researched on the internet about the ship and about Vasco da Gama.

A sailor who found the first sea route to India for trade, Da Gama was appointed the Viceroy of India. He was a renowned personality in the history of the world. He sailed to India twice and he died in India.

'It has definitely something to do with India. Da Gama has a brief history in India. The ship sank when it was sailing to India. What is the connection of the ship with Indians? What must it be?' said Neel to Jay when Jay brought some coffee for Neel.

'I don't know! The Omani said that they heard the thieves speaking in Hindi. But Hindi is spoken in major parts of Asia. We can't find the thief just by the language he speaks,' said Jay and grabbed a piece of pastry.

'Language matters. So you have deduced that the thief is a *he*? And why the hell are you eating a cake here?'

'I like it! And it's not a cake, it's a pastry,' said Jay.

'Oh, shut up! And why did you not bring one for me?'

'You want one? I thought you had killed the kid in you.'

'No, why would I? Bring a piece for me too!'

'I thought when Avantika left you, you had become a matured guy, but I was wrong! Wait, I will bring you one,' Jay said and went to the counter.

'You always manage to bring her up,' Neel muttered.

Neel and Jay sat in the plane when their flight was announced. Jay was preparing himself for the long journey. Neel sat silently in his seat and closed his eyes. He thought of the shipwreck and the artefacts. He also thought of the murder of Akash Gupta. But he drew no conclusions.

An airhostess arrived and told them to put on their seat belts.

'Isn't she beautiful?' Jay asked Neel.

'She can understand English,' said Neel.

'Why can't I get married to an airhostess?'

'Because you are a fool!'

'I am not a fool! After this trip, I promise I will get married.'

'And do what? Can't you see my condition?'

'Yes, but I am of age now.'

'Do whatever you want. Just don't give me a chance to call you a joker.'

'Fine! You will never understand my sentiments.'

The plane took off. Neel went into a deep sleep. Jay was looking over for some entertaining videos on his phone. He knew he had to spend the long twelve hours sitting at one place.

Lisbon, Portugal

The sun was about to rise. The first ray of sunshine was about to flash its light over the city when the plane landed in Lisbon. Neel and Jay were busy searching for Indian officers at the airport in Lisbon. The embassy had informed them that they'd send people to pick them at the airport. And then they saw some Indian faces holding a board on which their names were printed.

Neel and Jay went to them and greeted them.

'Welcome to Lisbon, sir!' said one of the officers.

'Thank you for picking us up,' said Neel. The trolley of bags was in Jay's control. He took the two bags and they started moving towards the gate.

'Rakesh sir will meet you at ten in the morning,' the officer said.

'Fine, how far is the hotel from here?' asked Neel.

'Sir, it can take half an hour to reach.'

'How far is the Indian Embassy?'

'Sir, it takes an hour to reach the Indian Embassy.'

'So, have you discussed the main purpose of my visit to Portugal?'

'Yes sir, the Indian ambassador has discussed the topic with the Portuguese ministry. The Portuguese are unaware about the incident and they say that they can't break their protocol and give us all the information.'

'Fine, let's see what happens.'

Neel and Jay reached the hotel and checked in into their respective suites. Neel glanced at his phone. The time was about 6 a.m. Neel decided to take a short nap. He put an alarm for 8 a.m. and lay down on the cozy bed.

His eyes were open and he looked at the ceiling. The beautiful white architecture fascinated him. He got up and glanced out of the window. The beautiful mansions with identical red roofs shined in the first rays of the sun.

Why isn't this in India? This is just beautiful!

He went back to the bed and lay down. He closed his eyes but was not at all feeling sleepy. He took out his cell phone and unlocked it. He then searched for his photos with Avantika. A photo that caught his eye was the one taken on his wedding day. The red sari Avantika was wearing illuminated when she smiled. The two looked perfect in the photo. When Neel had married Avantika, it had been like a dream come true for him.

I am such an idiot to lose her in this way!

He hated himself for losing Avantika. But according to him, he had no choice. He believed that destiny had made them part ways. But at the same time, he knew that Avantika would come back. He knew she would forgive him.

Lost in his thoughts, he dozed off. At 8 o'clock, the phone starting ringing. The soulful instrumental music that he had set for an alarm was not disturbing. He got up and put the alarm off.

After shaving off his light beard, he went for a bath. The hot water turned his body red. When he came out of the bathroom, he heard a knock on the door.

'Who's it?' Neel shouted from a distance.

Neel understood it was Jay. He said, 'Wait for a while.'

'How much time?' asked Jay.

'One hour!' Neel shouted looking for his clothes.

'Are you serious?'

'Yes,' said Neel when he found a shirt. *A fool will always be a fool!*

After wearing the clothes, Neel opened the door. Jay was standing leaning on the door. He got in and asked, 'What were you doing?'

'Getting ready,' said Neel combing his hair.

'You are late! The Indian ambassador will be meeting us at ten.'

'It's not even nine!' said Neel looking at the mirror with an eye on Jay.

'So, what will we do for an hour?' Jay said and sat on the bed. 'Isn't the bed really soft?'

'Yes, it is.'

'Can we go sightseeing after our work is over?' asked Jay in a low voice.

'Shut up! We are not here on a vacation,' Neel snapped.

'Fine! Then let's go and have breakfast,' said Jay and got up from the bed. He took out his phone and checked his emails.

The Indian ambassador, Rakesh Sharma, arrived at the hotel at 10 a.m.

'Good morning, Neel. I hope you like the hotel. How was your journey?'

'Yes, the hotel is wonderful. And the journey was good,' said Neel.

'The foreign ministry contacted us and informed us about the case. Then, I spoke with the police department and the foreign minister of Portugal.'

'What is their opinion about the matter? Do they have any information?' asked Neel.

'I don't think they have any information on it. But yes, they have put together a team to locate the artefacts.'

'Can I meet the officials?'

'Yes, I have organized a meeting with the foreign minister. We will visit him at 1 p.m.'

'Thank you for your co-operation,' said Neel.

'It's our duty, sir. I will be here to pick you up at twelve,' said Rakesh and stood up from his chair.

'We will be ready,' replied Neel. Rakesh nodded and started walking out of the hotel. Jay, who was sitting right next to Neel, stood up and sat in front of him, where Rakesh had been sitting.

'I don't understand anything. What must be the reason behind the robbery? And the main question is, who are the thieves? We haven't got any clue as yet,' said Jay.

'The main question is why they haven't contacted anyone for a deal,' replied Neel.

'What would they want?'

'That is what I am thinking,' said Neel. 'If they haven't done this for money or any deal, then it will be difficult to find them. It might be possible then that the matter may be related to the history of Vasco da Gama.'

'We should read up the history. The history of the ship and of Da Gama and also that of his uncle, who was the sailor of the ship.'

'Find out about Da Gama in Portugal. Find out the things related to Da Gama in Portugal.'

'There is a bridge in Lisbon named Vasco da Gama Bridge. There are monuments and there is a hotel.'

'I am sure the Portuguese must have documents related to him.'

'Yes, but they would never reveal them to us. It is the matter of international security. We won't get access to them.'

'Yes, but we will have to try!' Neel said and stood up. He went into his suite and researched about Vasco da Gama on his phone.

At about ten minutes to 12, he came out of his suite and went to get Jay. Jay was ready when Neel knocked on the door.

'C'mon, Rakesh is waiting outside,' said Neel.

'Yes,' said Jay and locked the door. They went into the lift and then to the reception. Jay submitted the card and they went out of the hotel.

After reaching the foreign ministry, Neel kept staring at the building for a long time. 'Anything wrong?' asked Rakesh.

'No, nothing! Just looking at the building,' replied Neel.

'It is an old building. It is marvelous! The police department and the foreign minister are present in the office,' said Rakesh.

'Let's go!' said Jay.

After entering the building, a portrait of Vasco da Gama caught Neel's eye. He stared at the portrait and tried to grab every minute detail. It was a portrait of the Portuguese sailor. He moved on and reached the office of the foreign minister of Portugal. They entered the office and Neel saw a Portuguese flag beside the minister's chair. The minister got up from his chair to shake hands with Rakesh and Neel. Jay was behind Neel, watching the formalities. They sat on the chairs and Rakesh started briefing the minister about the case. The minister knew a little English. However, the translator did most of the job. The minister seemed to be in his fifties. He listened to the case carefully. After Rakesh finished his part, the minister wasted no time to express himself.

'The shipwreck is an important discovery. But then, it is also connected to Portugal,' said the minister.

'Exactly sir, we wanted to know whether there has been any communication made to Portugal relating to the robbery?' asked Neel.

'No, we have no authorized information about the case. But yes, Portugal has sent its agents to investigate the case. It is important for us to find about the shipwreck.'

'The ship is believed to have been owned by Vasco da Gama. The missing artefacts are of importance. Do they have any specific history?'

'I will have to find out! We have friendly relations with India and we will help you in retrieving the artefacts. As we all know, Vasco da Gama was a key person in building the relation between India and Portugal. We will give the necessary information to India whenever it will become available to us,' the minister said.

'Thank you sir, for your personal attention in the matter,' said Neel.

After the meeting, the three of them sat in the car and made their way back to the hotel.

'I think a third party is involved in this robbery,' said Rakesh.

'Can't say. We will have to study the history associated,' said Neel.

'But it is possible that terrorists are involved in the robbery,' Rakesh said doubtfully.

'If it was a work of terrorists, they would have contacted someone for their demands. Or they would have taken responsibility of the robbery. There is no such sign from anyone. It is a work of a historian.'

'Yes, that makes sense,' Rakesh said nodding.

'Can I get a list of all historians in Portugal?'

'There are many people and it is difficult to get a complete list. But I will try to get one.'

'Jay, you contact Oman and tell them to make a list of all the historians. And tell them to send us a list of all the Indians and Portuguese who visited Oman before the robbery and after the robbery. From about a month before the robbery till date,' said Neel to Jay.

'Fine,' said Jay.

'And I need the same from you Rakesh,' said Neel.

'Yes, I will provide the lists as soon as possible,' said Rakesh.

'To carry out such a robbery, the real thief must have visited Oman at least once. We need to get the list of Indian people living in Oman. According to the Omani, the thieves spoke in Hindi and English. We also need to contact the embassies of Pakistan, Bangladesh, Nepal and Sri Lanka,' said Neel.

'What if we look into history and find out the countries visited by Vasco da Gama,' said Jay.

'Yes, I think we should do that too,' said Rakesh.

'Find out then,' said Neel to Jay. 'Also see if you can locate any Indian criminals in Oman. The mastermind must have hired a local team to do this work.'

'I think the Omani must be working in the direction,' said Jay.

'Tell them to notify us,' said Neel.

'It's really hard to find a criminal without any lead,' said Rakesh.

'But it's not impossible!' exclaimed Neel. 'Call Raghu and give him the report.'

Jay connected his call to India and updated Raghu.

'He says he wants to talk to you,' said Jay in between the call.

Neel took the phone and said, 'Yes, sir?'

'Neel, come back to India! We have new information. I will make all the arrangements for your departure from Lisbon.'

'Sure, sir. Please send me the details of the flight,' said Neel.

Neel was wondering what new information Raghu had. He knew he would now finally get a clue about the robbery.

'He said the flight is scheduled for tomorrow and he told us to land in Delhi as there is another mission abroad,' said Jay.

'Fine!' said Neel.

'But there's one problem.'

'What?' Neel looked up, curious.

'He told me that Avantika will also be there in Delhi for the meeting.'

'What? But she had resigned! Is she ready for a meeting?' asked Neel with a shocked face.

'I don't know, but I think Raghu is insisting that she is present.'

Neel touched his forehead with his fingers. He said nothing and glanced out of the window. The moving road and the passing of the houses reminded him of an incident. He went back to the past and brooded over the scene.

Neel and Avantika were in the car. The driver was driving the car and they both were sitting on the back seat. She had put her head on Neel's shoulder. Neel was looking out of the window towards the sea. They were in Goa. The sea was silent and calm in its own noise.

'Avantika, look at the sea! Should we go there?' said Neel rolling his hand over her head.

She looked up and glanced at the sea. 'Yes, I want to walk with you on the coastline!' She was excited.

When they reached the coast, Neel and Avantika started walking hand in hand on the shore. They clicked selfies in different poses. She held Neel's hand and came close to him. She lay her head on his shoulder.

'I love you my dear hubby,' she said in a low voice.

'I love you too, my moon,' Neel said and looked deep into her eyes.

They were enjoying their love. Their eyes had fallen in love. The blue sky above them, the brown sand below, the blue ocean in front and the two deeply in love. The only thing that was missing was a light shower of rain.

Neel came back into his senses when he heard the long beep of the horn. They had reached the hotel. After their formal greetings, Neel went into his suite. He had nothing to do but wait. He had to wait for more than twenty-four hours to finally see Avantika. He was not ready for the union.

What should I do? How should I react? Will she forgive me?

Neel was confused. He had not seen Avantika for months. He had not even heard her beautiful voice for months. He forcefully tried to distract his mind from her. He took the file of the case and started looking for a clue in the photos. He studied the photos carefully and marked some of them.

Neel and Jay were at the Lisbon International Airport. After their flight was announced, they moved towards the departure. Taking their seats, Neel finally relaxed. He was preparing himself to face Avantika.

After the long twelve-hour journey, finally they reached the Delhi airport. Two officers greeted them, and they headed towards the parking lot. It was night time. After getting into the car, Neel asked one of the officers, 'Who else is at the hotel?'

Jay looked at Neel and gave a smile. He knew Neel was itching to meet Avantika.

'Raghu and the other officers,' replied the officer.

'Is Avantika at the hotel?' Neel asked specifically.

'Yes, she is at the hotel. She will be attending the meeting tomorrow.'

'Fine,' said Neel and went into deep thought.

They reached the hotel and went into their respective rooms. Neel kept his bag and sat on the bed with a deep sigh. He closed his eyes and touched them with his fingers.

Oh god! What a mess you have put me into.

He began imagining different ways to meet her. Then, finally, he dialled Jay's number.

'Jay, come to my room. I need to talk,' said Neel.

When Jay entered the room, Neel was sweating. Jay noticed his discomfort and said, 'Don't worry, I met her.'

'What? Are you serious?' Neel asked in shock.

'Yes,' Jay said and sat on the couch.

'What did she say? How is she?' Neel asked without a pause.

'Nothing, she's fine. She asked me about you.'

'What did you say?'

'I told her that you are fine.'

'I am sure you must have added a few lines too.'

'No, not at all.'

'Fine, thank you,' said Neel.

After sleeping well, Neel got up early in the morning. He got ready before time. He was excited for his meeting with Avantika.

Neel and Jay reached the headquarters. They went to meet Raghu. He told them to gather in the meeting hall. After a while, as the meeting was about to start, Jay and Neel took their places. In a short while, Raghu entered the room and behind him entered Avantika.

Neel saw her and gave no reaction. She was wearing a red sari and looked beautiful enough to make Neel fall in love with her again.

'We have got new information on the Oman case,' said Raghu.

He gave a file to Neel and said, 'Two days ago, Shivam Saran's wife told the police that her husband was missing. We have traced that Shivam is in Oman. Our intelligence agency has information that he was seen in Oman. You three will have to go and find out the truth behind the murder. Also find about the shipwreck in Oman.'

Three? Who is the third person?

After the meeting, Neel and Jay came out of the meeting room.

'Who is the third person? Who was he talking about?'

'It's Avantika! Raghu wants her to accompany us in the mission,' said Jay in a low voice.

'And? Is she ready?'

'No! She told me that she doesn't want to work with you.'

'I knew that. Leave it!'

'And what about Oman and Shivam? Why is he in Oman? I think he is there to make a movie on the discovery of the shipwreck,' said Jay.

'I don't know!' replied Neel. He saw Avantika heading towards them and got away from there. He went and sat in the car.

After a while, Jay called Neel on his phone and said, 'Neel, come back! Avantika is here. She wants to talk to you.'

'What? Are you sure?' Neel got confused. He got out of the car and walked towards the office. He saw Jay and Avantika standing at a distance.

'Why did you tell Raghu to appoint me on the mission?' asked Avantika.

'What? I? I did not tell him anything,' said Neel, confused.

'This is a misunderstanding. Neel did not tell Raghu about you,' said Jay.

'Then? Who was it?' asked Avantika.

'It was me!' replied Jay.

'What?' Avantika was shocked.

'Are you mad?' shouted Neel.

'I am sorry,' said Jay. 'I just wanted you both to be together.'

'It's not possible,' said Avantika and left the place. She did not forget to look into Neel's eyes. She was embarrassed, but she had faith in Neel. She was angry, but she could not stop herself from showing her satisfaction on seeing Neel.

'Are you crazy? Why did you do that?' shouted Neel.

'I am sorry,' Jay said in a low voice.

'You are making it worse,' said Neel and left the place.

The Delhi meeting ended with disappointment for Neel. Neel, Jay, Avantika and Raghu returned to Chennai.

Neel reached home. The house was dark and lonely. He kept his stuff and lay down on the bed. He closed his eyes and the smiling face of Avantika came before him. He opened his eyes and it vanished. The phenomenon continued. Her smiling face changed into a sad face gradually. He had met Avantika after a long time. He recalled all the words she said at the Delhi meeting. He was disturbed. He did not want Avantika to be uncomfortable because of him. He decided to tell Raghu about it. The next day, he went to meet Raghu.

As usual, Raghu was busy with his work. At times, Neel thought how Raghu managed to handle both, office and family. He thought of asking him about it, but could not. He sat on the chair in Raghu's office. Raghu was busy talking to someone on his phone. He kept his phone aside after some time.

'Yes Neel. Sorry to keep you waiting. So how does it feel to work with Avantika again?' said Raghu.

'Sir, I think it will be uncomfortable for Avantika to work with me,' said Neel, avoiding eye contact.

'No Neel, she will be fine! You solve your disputes and work together. Every relation may have problems, but separation is not the correct solution,' explained Raghu. He understood Neel's discomfort but still had hope for him.

'But, sir...' Neel said and paused.

'I will talk about it with Avantika. She will be okay. Leave it to me. You have to go with her. I will hear nothing more from you both. You have this golden chance to repair your relation,' declared Raghu with an air of finality.

Neel could do nothing. Now, he had to go with Avantika for the mission. Avantika too would have to listen to Raghu. He was not sure, but there was definitely a ray of hope and happiness and he looked forward to it.

At last, the day arrived when Neel, Jay and Avantika had to leave for Muscat. The flight was at night. Jay had fixed a cab and told Neel and Avantika that he would pick them both from their respective homes. Jay was clever enough to pick Neel first. After picking up Neel, they both headed towards Avantika's house. Jay saw Neel's awkwardness as they were nearing her house gradually. As soon as they reached her house, Neel started fidgeting. Jay came out of the car and called Avantika. He suddenly opened the door of the front seat.

'I will sit in the front,' he said slowly. 'You both sit together in the back seat.'

Neel completely forgot about the seat. He opened the door and was about to tell Jay to get back to the back seat when he sensed Avantika behind him. He turned and saw Avantika. She looked beautiful in the street light. She saw Neel. Their eyes met. Everything stopped for a while. Her skin was glowing. Neel was just looking at her and enjoying the moment.

'I would keep looking at you like this my entire life,' his eyes said. But then he tore his eyes away to the bag in her hand. Jay pinched him on his back. Neel went and took the bag from her hand. At first, she resisted, but eventually gave the bag to Neel and they got into the car. Neel sat next to her. Jay had a cute smile on his face. Neel and Avantika had stuck their heads out of their respective windows, though none of them saw what was outside the car.

'You excited Avantika?' Jay broke the ice.

'Shut up!' responded Avantika.

'I went to Muscat a few days ago. It's a beautiful and romantic place,' said Jay. Another attempt.

'Jay, will you please keep quiet,' said Neel, politely.

Jay remained silent. The distance increased. Not between them, but between them and the airport as well.

After a while, they reached the Chennai International Airport. Neel and Avantika did not talk to each other. Jay tried to entertain them. He made several attempts to make them talk, but in vain.

They were at the airport waiting for their departure. Suddenly, Neel's phone rang. He took it out from his pocket and saw it was Raghu.

'Neel, all the arrangements have been done. The details of the bank transactions of Shivam in Oman have been sent to Oman. You will definitely get a clue with that,' said Raghu.

'Yes sir, I will investigate.'

'And it is a good chance for you to improve your relation with Avantika. Tell her the truth and I am sure she will forgive you.'

'I will try to, sir.'

Jay was staring at Neel. He knew what Raghu must have told Neel. Avantika was silent and sitting next to Jay. Grabbing the right chance, Jay said, 'Hey, we will have to coordinate! We are together and we have an assignment to complete.'

'Will you just shut up!' exclaimed Neel.

'Can't we keep our personal issues aside when we are on an assignment?' replied Jay.

'I don't have any problem and I will give my best to the mission,' said Avantika. 'But there's only one condition...that you will not talk about my personal issues or my relation with Neel.'

Neel heard his name and the soft part of the heart softened further. He said in a low voice, 'I too have no problem in working with you both. And I too have the same condition that Avantika has.'

Avantika heard her name and smiled. She hid her face so that Neel would not notice it. But Neel had his eye on her. He saw her smile and smiled in return. Jay was enjoying the scene and he joined the smiling session as well.

Muscat, Oman

After reaching the Muscat airport, the three went to the hotel. Neel and Avantika were still hiding their faces from each other. And Jay was trying to make them talk.

They checked into their respective suites. Neel carried not only his luggage but hers too. He helped her in every possible way, but did not utter a word. She too liked it, but was silent. She waited for Neel to break the ice.

It was late at night and the three had separate suites on the same floor. Without having much of a conversation, they retired to bed.

The next day, a meeting with the Omani officials was arranged. They met at the hotel cafeteria. Avantika sat right in front of Neel, Jay to his left and the officer to his right.

'Can we have the address of Shivam in Oman?' Neel asked the officer.

'No, we are still trying to find it from the bank. We will get the address in a short while,' replied the officer.

'Is he alone? Or is someone accompanying him?' asked Avantika.

'Madam, according to flight details, he has travelled alone. But we are locating all the Indian people who travelled to Oman in the last few months.'

'Fine, and also, we will need a local body on this case. We will also have to find its relation with the shipwreck case,' said Neel.

'I think the cases are inter-related,' said Avantika.

'Can't say! But why would anyone be interested in the artefacts? What are they to do with the suicide of Akash?' commented Neel, avoiding eye contact with Avantika.

'Anything is possible! Anyone can betray anyone, for anything,' replied Avantika with a serious face, this time staring right into Neel's eyes. Neel looked at her for a fraction of a second and then looked away. He knew what she was trying to say. Jay saw her and smiled.

'Only when one is left with an inevitable choice,' said Neel.

'The choice itself says it's a choice,' commented Avantika, more serious this time.

As soon as Avantika said that, Jay cleared his throat to bring back Neel and Avantika to the matter at hand.

'Well, we will investigate that and find the real culprit,' said Jay.

After the meeting was over, Neel was alone, sitting on a couch in his suite. He was thinking about Avantika's words and was trying to figure out what was in her heart. Suddenly, his phone rang. It was the Omani officer.

'Neel, we have traced Shivam's address. I think we should go and check it out,' said the officer.

'Great! Text me the address and we will reach the place. You keep a local team with you because we do not exactly know what we could face,' replied Neel.

Neel called Jay and told him to inform Avantika about the address. After getting ready, the three of them headed out.

They reached the address. It was a bungalow which Shivam had taken on lease. The Omani police were already there. Neel and Jay went inside the bungalow. Neel went into the bedroom. A body was lying flat on the floor. The floor was red with blood. A chair had been overturned on the floor. Neel went close to the body. He saw a piece of paper in the pocket of the shirt. Seeing whether anyone was watching him, he took out the paper and kept it in his pocket.

He scanned the room and found a map lying on a table. He went and took the map. He folded it so that it would fit in his pocket.

'It's Shivam!' exclaimed Neel, when he saw Jay entering the room.

The Omani officer entered the room, went close to Neel, and told him, 'We have a suspect!'

'Who is it? And who killed Shivam? He has been stabbed!' said Jay.

The Omani officer said, 'Come and see the suspect.'

Neel and Jay went with him out of the bungalow. The suspect was in the police car. Neel went closer to see the suspect. As soon as he saw the suspect, he exclaimed, 'You!'

Jay too went near the car and said, 'How can it be him?'

'I don't know. We will have to interrogate him,' said Neel puzzled.

Neel went to his car and sat on the front seat. Avantika was standing near the car. She went to Neel and asked, 'Who was it?'

'Shankar Deo, the script writer,' replied Neel.

'Is Shivam dead?' asked Avantika.

'Yes, Shankar has admitted that he stabbed Shivam,' said Jay.

They went to the police headquarters and the police put Shankar in a cell.

'Can we interrogate him?' Neel asked to the officer.

'Yes, but later,' replied the officer.

'Why did he kill Shivam? Did he say anything?' asked Neel.

'Yes, we have got very crucial information. We will give the final report tomorrow. First we will have to interrogate him and extract all the information. We will call you when it's done.'

Jay and Avantika had to return to the hotel empty-handed unlike Neel who had a map and a mysterious piece of paper with him.

Neel went into his suite quietly. He took out the map and the paper. He unfolded the map. It was a world map. It had uneven markings on it such as circles, triangles and squares on it. He could not understand the meaning of the markings. The markings were all over the map. After trying hard to trace the markings, he kept the map aside. He took the paper out and saw it. It had a word written on it in capital letters. The word didn't make any sense. It had no meaning and no right pronunciation.

Neel took two photos, one of the map and the other of the paper. He researched on internet about the word, but ended up getting more confused. He quickly put the map and the paper in the drawer as he heard a knock on the door.

When he opened the door, he couldn't believe who it was. A ray of hope ran through his body. Words did not come out of his mouth.

'Y…you…' was all Neel could manage to stammer.

'Can I come in?' said the female voice.

'Yes, of course! You can…' replied Neel and moved aside.

'Can I sit down?'

'Yes, what brought you here?' asked Neel, confused and equally shocked.

'I wanted to talk to you.'

'I think the Omani police will give us the detailed report tomorrow.'

'It's not about that. It's about us.'

'What about us? I don't understand, Avantika,' said Neel and avoided eye contact.

'Do you feel what you did was a mistake? Don't you feel sorry? Are you happy living this way?'

'No, but are you ready to hear me out? Last time when I tried to tell you the truth, you spoiled my shirt with the coffee,' said Neel.

'So? Are you angry at me because of the shirt? Should I get you a new shirt? Shouldn't I be angry at you for what you did? Don't I have the right to spoil your shirt? And that too, only one shirt!' said Avantika looking straight into Neel's eyes. She knew Neel would never make eye contact.

'I did not say that.'

'Why didn't you contact me after that? I was angry, I was hurt. But it was your responsibility to tell me the truth. What I saw was real. You have to admit it. But I am sure you must have a good reason for that. I know you very well. Now, I want to know the reason. Why did you cheat on me?'

'I did not cheat on you. I did not cheat on anyone,' protested Neel.

'So, what was it? Are you trying to say that what I saw was unreal?'

'No, it was true! But your perspective was wrong.'

'What perspective Neel? I clearly saw you and the woman together. And that too in our bedroom! What else was left to be seen?'

'Yes, you saw us! But what were we doing? Do you know anything about what I was doing?'

'You were hugging her. In *our* bedroom! How will you explain that?'

'I was hugging her but that doesn't mean I was having an affair with her. But I should tell you that, yes, I was indeed having an affair with her.'

'So that's it! Are you confessing?' said Avantika and a tear dropped from her eye. Neel too, had tears in his eyes.

'A false affair! I had to do that. Believe me, it was all planned. I can prove that I did not have any choice and I was helpless.'

'How can a man be helpless about an affair? When you have a wife and you say you love her, what was your need for an affair? Can you explain that to me?'

'The truth is that the situation was tough. I was bound and I had to keep it secret. I could not even share it with you. I was going to tell you everything when it all was over. But unfortunately, you saw me and you left.'

'What should I have done then? What should I do now?'

'You are right! I have cheated on you. But I need to tell you the truth. And then it's your choice whether you want to leave me or stay with me. I am ready for everything!'

'I want to know!' commanded Avantika.

18 months ago...

It was Avantika's first day in the Chennai Police department. She had been transferred from Mumbai to Chennai. She had applied for a transfer to her hometown, Chennai. The department was kind to her and respected her. She worked hard and had acquired many medals for her work.

Neel was in the same department. He was the most awarded person in the department and the most stylish IPS officer in the batch. Neel was senior to Avantika in the department.

That day, as usual, Neel was in the office early in the morning. Jay was with Neel and they were discussing a case. Neel heard a knock on the door and he said, 'Yes, come in!'

'Sir, my name is Avantika and I am here to report in the office,' said Avantika.

'Oh! You have been transferred from Mumbai, right?'

'Yes sir,' she replied.

'Fine,' said Neel and told Jay to help her with the registration. 'Nice to meet you,' said Neel. He had never seen such a beautiful police officer till date.

When Jay entered the cabin, he said, 'She is beautiful.'

'Yes, did you show her the cabin?'

'Yes, don't worry. I never miss out on helping beautiful women.'

While discussing the case, Raghu entered Neel's cabin.

'Neel and Jay, you will have to work with the new officer! She is new here and I am sure you guys can understand her better,' said Raghu.

'Yes sir,' said Neel.

'You three will be working in a same department and you will have to tackle the undercover missions.'

Suddenly, Avantika entered the cabin and Raghu introduced her to Neel and Jay. The feeling Neel was trying to avoid was dying to sprout out.

After the discussion, Neel and Avantika got busy with their work. In the evening when leaving the office, Neel saw Avantika and went close to her.

'You can contact me if you need something. I can understand, it may be hard for you adjusting to a new place,' said Neel.

'No, actually Chennai is my hometown. I got transferred here because I was uncomfortable in Mumbai,' replied Avantika.

'Oh, I thought you were from Mumbai,' said Neel.

The conversation had begun. Neel took her address as well as her phone number. She too did not hesitate to take Neel's address and number. She too was feeling attracted towards Neel.

From the next day, as ordered by Raghu, they started working together. The assignments brought them close and kept them in frequent contact. They started to know each other and also began getting attracted towards each other. They also met in public places and started enjoying time with each other.

No doubt, Jay understood that Neel and Avantika were enjoying each other's presence. He too felt that Avantika was the right person for Neel. The other officers soon noticed the ongoing attraction as well.

One fine day, Neel went to drop Avantika at her home, as he usually did. They were in the car and the music player was playing a romantic song. They were engaged in a conversation related to a case. At one moment, both of them paused. The song made its way to their hearts. Neel suddenly started concentrating on the lyrics. So did Avantika.

'So? Have you any plans of marrying?' asked Neel.

'No, not yet! The police job doesn't give me time to think about it. And I haven't met any person who would accept me as I am,' replied Avantika.

'Why? What's wrong with you?'

'Nothing specially, but police officers need a police person,' said Avantika and smiled. Neel too smiled, satisfied with her statement.

'So you want a policeman?' said Neel and laughed.

'What about you? Haven't you thought about marriage?' asked Avantika.

'No, not yet! When the right time comes, I will.'

'And when will it be the right time?'

'Don't know! But probably when I fall in love.'

'So a police guy is romantic,' Avantika said and smiled.

'Not really, but just want to fall in love at least once.'

'Love happens only once Neel,' commented Avantika and became serious. Neel heard her words and became quiet. No one spoke for a moment.

After dropping Avantika off, Neel went home. That night, he started thinking of Avantika seriously. He knew that he had fallen in love. He knew Avantika had fallen in love with him too. But he feared speaking to her about it.

A few days later, one evening, Neel decided to propose to her. After their work at the office, as usual, Neel told her that he would drop her home. They left the office and started for her house. The main challenge for Neel was to ask her out for coffee.

'So, what...' said Neel and paused.

'What?' asked Avantika, looking at Neel.

'How was your day?' asked Neel.

'I was with you the entire day. Don't you know how our day was?'

'Yes, I am tired,' said Neel and switched on the radio in the car.

The radio understood Neel's feelings very well. The romantic song filled the car with its soulful tune.

'I am tired too. I need sleep!' said Avantika and lowered the volume of the radio.

'How about some coffee?' asked Neel.

'Now?' Avantika said with hesitation.

'Yes, you will feel better,' said Neel making an excuse.

'But...'

'Oh c'mon Avantika,' protested Neel.

'Fine,' said Avantika and a smile appeared on Neel's face.

Avantika saw him smile. 'Why are you smiling?' she asked.

'Nothing.'

They reached the coffee shop which Neel had selected. He had already told the owner of the coffee shop about the plan. The coffee shop was empty as planned. They sat on the table, which Neel had asked them to decorate. Avantika was amazed but still didn't suspect anything.

Neel picked up the roses which were kept on the table. He went down on his knees and proposed to her. She was speechless and clearly shocked.

'I love you Avantika! Will you marry me?'

Avantika had tears in her eyes. Neel saw the tears and got up. She hugged him tightly. Neel tried to calm her down.

'I love you Neel! Thank you for asking me,' she said into his ears.

A smile appeared on Neel's face. Avantika smiled and Neel wiped her tears. The owner of the coffee shop and the other staff clapped. Suddenly, Jay and Raghu entered the coffee shop. Avantika was shocked to see them. Everyone congratulated them.

'So you had it planned,' said Avantika blushing.

Neel said nothing and smiled. 'I loved it!' said Avantika.

'I am happy for both of you,' said Raghu. He had brought a gift for them. He gave it to Neel and Avantika.

'It's so kind of you,' said Avantika.

'What is it?' asked Neel.

'You will have to open it to see,' said Raghu.

Neel removed the wrapping paper. He opened the box. It was a statue of a couple with their hands in each other's, looking into each other's eyes.

'It's wonderful!' said Avantika.

'Just like you both,' said Raghu.

'I too have a gift for you,' said Jay. He removed two small boxes from his pocket and handed one to Neel and one to Avantika.

'Is it a ring?' asked Avantika.

'Yes, you guessed it right!' said Jay.

Jay gifted a ring to Neel and a ring to Avantika.

'Now you will have to give each other the rings. It was very difficult for me to find the perfect ring for you both,' said Jay.

They slipped the rings on each other's fingers.

'Thank you Jay. But why did you spend so much?' asked Avantika.

'Oh, no problem. Do not worry about that. Anything for you both.'

'Thank you Jay,' said Neel.

The evening ended happily. They all had dinner together. Neel and Avantika were happy, and Raghu and Jay were happy for them. They discussed future plans. Raghu and Jay told them to get married as soon as possible.

They laughed and they enjoyed themselves. The party ended. Neel dropped Avantika home. They reached her house and Neel came out of the car to walk her to the door. She came out of the car and held Neel's hand. She said nothing.

'Thank you Avantika for accepting me,' said Neel, looking deep into her eyes.

'Thank *you* for asking me! I am happy for us. I want you to be my husband. I want you in my life till the end of mine,' said Avantika.

'I promise I will be with you, no matter what,' said Neel and hugged her.

That night, Neel and Avantika slept well. They were away from each other but still connected. That day marked the official beginning of their relationship.

They went to office together the next day. He then dropped her home, which became a routine for every day. On some occasions, they went to the beach in Chennai to spend time together. Then they decided to inform their parents and get married. Their parents were only too happy. They planned everything for the wedding together. They shopped together and chose each other's outfits. Neel picked a red sari for her. And Avantika picked a sherwani for Neel. They were very happy.

The marriage date drew close. Neel, Jay and Avantika made all the arrangements. And finally, the day arrived. The marriage was set on a beach-side resort in Chennai. Avantika looked beautiful in the red sari. Everyone was waiting for her as she arrived at the wedding venue. Jay stood next to Neel.

'She is looking so beautiful! This is the best version of her till date. This is the first time she is not looking like a police officer,' Neel told Jay.

'Yes, you are lucky! You have got a beautiful wife,' said Jay.

'Thank you Jay. I just can't wait to marry her,' said Neel and smiled. Jay smiled back.

'Enjoy your wedding boss,' said Jay grinning.

Avantika arrived and stood in front of Neel. He stood staring at her.

'You are looking wonderful… so gorgeous,' said Neel softly.

Avantika smiled and said, 'Shut up! You too are looking rather handsome.'

'Will you marry me?' asked Neel.

'And what am I doing right now?'

'Come with me. We will run away! I don't want people staring at you,' said Neel. Avantika smiled.

'Shut up and concentrate.'

They were happy and they enjoyed their wedding. They were finally married. They had their honeymoon in Goa to look forward to next.

They had booked a beach resort in Goa. The resort had a private swimming pool. The sea facing swimming pool amazed them.

'It's so beautiful. I love this place!' said Avantika when they were checking out the resort.

'Yes, it's beautiful. I have a plan,' said Neel smiling.

'What plan?' asked Avantika.

'Today evening, we will put up a chair near the pool and enjoy the evening.'

'Yes, it's so calm here and so romantic!'

They had a candle light dinner and then had fun in the pool.

'Neel, I love you! You are the best person in my life,' said Avantika. She was sitting next to Neel on a chair.

'You are copying my dialogue Avantika,' said Neel.

'Shut up!'

'I think we need something. A bottle of wine.'

'I don't drink!'

'Nor do I, but the waiter told me he has a great bottle of wine. Let's try it!'

'Are you sure?'

'Yes don't worry,' said Neel and ordered the wine.

The waiter filled two glasses. Neel gave a glass to Avantika and took one for himself. They took their glasses but Avantika just stared at her glass.

'C'mon, drink it,' said Neel and made her drink some from his glass.

She grimaced but she liked it. Neel started laughing when he saw her face. He drank his wine and Avantika laughed loudly when she saw him making a face.

'It's good. You liked it?' asked Neel.

'Yes, it is good. You make me do terrible things,' she said and emptied her glass. Neel was staring at her in a shock. When she kept her glass back on the table she said, 'What? Why are you staring?'

'Nothing! You are amazing,' said Neel and laughed aloud.

'You still haven't finished yours,' said Avantika pointing at his glass.

'Yes, I am trying to.'

Avantika got up from her chair. She grabbed his glass and kept it back on the table.

'What are you doing? I haven't finished the wine.'

She said nothing. She went close to him and sat on his lap. She went close to his face, put her hands on his shoulders and kissed him.

Neel kissed her back. He got up from his place, grabbed her in his arms and went inside their bedroom. The lights were turned off. But the light of the love was still burning.

The next morning, Avantika got up first. Neel was right next to her. She saw his face and kissed him on his cheek.

'You look more handsome in the morning,' she said to herself.

She got up and ordered some coffee. Neel got up and did not find Avantika by his side. He got up and went to the pool. He saw her standing and watching the sea. He walked up to her.

'Good morning wife,' said Neel and kissed her on her forehead.

'Good morning Neel. My head!'

'You did not sleep well?'

'No, I mean yes, but my head is just bursting.'

'I will order coffee.'

'I already did!'

'So we will order some medicine.'

He hugged her. The morning sunshine was making her skin glow. The breeze from the sea brought the moisture in. The coffee arrived and they went inside. They had the coffee and Neel ordered the medicines.

'What do we do today?' asked Avantika.

'Just sit here and sleep all day. This place is so wonderful, I don't feel like leaving it,' said Neel.

'We are on a holiday, my dear husband. When I feel better, I am going to drag you with me!'

'But why? Can't we just stay here? I mean, look how beautiful this place is! The sunrise and the sunset can be clearly seen from here. The sea is right in front of us. What else do we need?' said Neel.

'We are on a holiday, Neel! You are going to stay in this room the entire holiday?'

'Of course not! I was just kidding. You think I would keep you in this room?' said Neel, smiling.

'Yes, get ready! I am feeling better now. Let's explore some places,' said Avantika. She got up and hugged Neel.

'Yes, get ready,' said Neel and hugged her back.

'What should I wear? Pink or red?'

'There's not much difference. Both are same,' said Neel.

'Pick one.'

'Red, if it's comfortable,' said Neel, slowly.

'Fine! And what are you going to wear? Don't wear the dull clothes you wear at office,' said Avantika.

'I am a police officer!'

'So? You don't have the right to look handsome?'

'Yes, I do.'

'There is a surprise for you. I bought you some clothes! Throw away your old ones. From now, you will wear only what I want to see you in.'

'Thanks for the clothes,' said Neel pleasantly surprised. Avantika showed him the gifts she had bought. Neel liked them all. Even if he hadn't liked them, he really had no choice but to wear them.

They enjoyed their vacation exploring much of Goa. They visited the old churches, beaches, and all the touristy places. Their trip was short but filled with sweet memories.

Soon they got back to work and began to balance their personal and professional lives. One fine day, Raghu appointed Neel on a secret mission. Jay was aware of the mission too.

'The drug dealer Roshan supplies all the drugs from south India to Goa and north India. He also runs a land development firm. Recently he has been spotted in Chennai, but we don't have enough proof against him,' said Raghu.

'So how does he carry out the drugs dealing? How can we get to him?'

'He has a girlfriend! He loves her, but she does not love him. You will have to get to her and extract all the information against Roshan. I am sure she will help you,' replied Raghu.

'Sir, but I am a married person now . . . what if Avantika gets to know?'

'You will have to work secretly! We cannot leak the information. I know it's not right, but you have to do this. When the work is completed, I will inform Avantika about it, don't worry.'

Neel had no option but to obey Raghu's orders. He knew it was not right. He knew Avantika would get to know one day. But he had faith in Raghu and he had faith in himself.

When Neel got all the information on the case, he started visiting Roshan's construction sites. He found nothing there.

'Roshan's girlfriend, Richa, goes jogging every day near her house and then she goes to the gym. That's the only time you can get close to her,' said Jay.

'Fine! We will join the gym and go jogging from tomorrow.'

'We?' asked Jay.

'Yes, we both,' said Neel.

The next morning, as planned, Neel and Jay went jogging on the ground close to Richa's house. Neel had her photo in his phone. His eyes searched for Richa everywhere. And there she was! Richa was jogging with headphones in her ears. Her slim body and the slim fit tracksuit attracted Jay.

'Wow! She is beautiful,' commented Jay.

'So, how to start? She is a model, right?'

'Yes, she is a beautiful model. But she has stopped working now.'

'No problem, you go and talk to her. Tell her she is beautiful and you saw her on magazine covers,' said Neel.

Jay did as Neel said. Neel was watching them from a distance. After a moment, Neel went towards her and said, 'Oh, hi! You are Richa, right?'

'Ya, I thought people have forgotten me,' said Richa smiling.

'No, not at all! You look beautiful. Why did you leave modelling?'

'Actually, I had to. Some personal issues . . .'

'Anyway, nice to meet you! I am Neel; I am a civil engineer and am planning to start a construction site in this area.'

'Oh great! My boyfriend has construction sites in the city too.'

'Oh really? Then it will be nice to meet him,' said Neel.

'Ya, but he is a very busy person. He is not in the city now.'

'Fine, no problem. Glad to meet you! And I must say that he is lucky to have such a beautiful girlfriend.'

'I really appreciate that, thank you.'

After the conversation, Neel and Jay followed her to the gym. Richa was surprised to see Neel and Jay again. They ended up having a long conversation. Neel noticed that she was lonely. Roshan did not give her much time and imposed many restrictions on her.

The daily visits got Neel close to Richa. Avantika was totally unaware of the ongoing mission. Richa was opening up to Neel. She gradually revealed her hardships. She also revealed that she did not love Roshan. They were not married yet.

One fine day, when Richa and Neel were at the gym, Neel started asking her some personal questions.

'Why did you leave modelling?'

'Roshan doesn't like it. And I can't hurt him.'

'Do you really love him?'

'Yes . . . I love him. He too loves me,' she said, more to herself.

'What kind of business does he have? Other than construction?'

'He has many kinds of business! He doesn't tell me much.'

'You say you love him and he too loves you, then how did he not tell you about his work?'

'No, it's not that! He doesn't like to speak of his work at home.'

'Are you afraid of him?'

'No, why will I be afraid? But actually, I am afraid *for* him.'

'Afraid for him? Why? Any problem?'

'His work has led to many rivals! And some of the work is illegal. That's why I am afraid!'

'Why illegal?'

'I don't know specifically. C'mon, let's go! I have to go home,' she said and left.

Neel had extracted a certain amount of information from her. On the other hand, he felt sorry for her.

A few days later, one afternoon, when Neel was at home and Avantika was out shopping, he got a call from Richa.

'Hello, Neel! Where are you? I want to meet you right now,' said Richa. She seemed afraid and was crying.

'What happened? Are you alright?'

'Just meet me now. Where are you?'

'I am at home . . .'

'Fine, I am coming there,' she said and ended the call.

Neel could not utter a word. Neel had given her his address. He had also lied to her that he was single.

A few minutes later, he heard the doorbell. He saw it was Richa. As soon as Neel opened the door, Richa hugged Neel and started crying. Neel's discomfort was totally visible on his face.

'What's wrong Richa? What happened?' asked Neel and pushed her aside. Her cheeks were red, as if someone had slapped her hard.

'Roshan! He is not a good person, Neel. I hate him.'

'What did he do? Tell me what happened.'

'He slapped me. I told him that I want to go out with my friends. He said 'no'.He has put so many restrictions on me. I had a fight with him and he slapped me,' said Richa sobbing.

'Don't worry, we will inform the police.'

'No, he is a very powerful person! He will kill me if I contact the police.'

'He will do nothing to you! Don't worry. I have some friends in the police. I will handle the matter.'

Neel tried to console her. She was crying hysterically. After that, Richa went to wash her face in the attached bathroom. Neel guided her. When she was back, she hugged Neel and said, 'Thank you so much Neel.'

Avantika had the keys of the front door. She was back from shopping and had opened the door and entered the house. She heard a female voice from the bedroom. She went towards the bedroom and saw Neel and Richa hugging each other.

'Who is she?' said Richa when she saw Avantika.

Neel was stunned to see Avantika staring at them in shock. Avantika did not utter a word and walked out of the house. Neel cried out her name, but she did not respond.

'She is my wife,' said Neel to Richa.

'But you said you were single.'

'I am sorry, I lied,' said Neel. He went and followed Avantika, but she was gone.

Richa too was hurt and she too left. Neel was all alone in the house. He tried to call Avantika, but she did not pick up his call. Then he called Jay and told him about the incident.

'Don't worry, I will call Avantika and explain everything to her,' said Jay.

'Do one more thing! Call Richa and tell her to lodge an FIR against Roshan. Add a case of domestic violence. Arrest him and then we will be able to interrogate him,' said Neel.

After the call, Neel called Avantika. This time she picked up the call.

'Avantika, please come home! I can explain. It was not real. Please come home!' cried Neel.

'Why? Why Neel? Why?' Avantika said sobbing.

'At least listen to me! Don't believe what you saw. Let me explain please!'

'No, Neel! I can't listen to you now. I am coming home, but don't try to stop me! I am going back to my parents,' she said and ended the call.

After a while, she came home. Neel was sitting on the couch and waiting for her. As soon as he saw Avantika, he got up and said, 'Avantika, just give me one chance! I can explain!'

'Explain what? That you are having an affair. And it was by mistake?'

'No, it was not by mistake. Avantika, just be calm and please listen to me,' said Neel.

Avantika was not in the mood to listen to Neel. She was terribly hurt. She saw a coffee mug on the table. The coffee was still in the mug. She took the coffee mug and threw the coffee on Neel's red shirt.

'Just get lost! I am leaving,' she screamed.

Neel was silent. He did not utter a word. Avantika went to the bedroom, took her clothes, packed them and went off. Neel saw Avantika going but did not say anything.

After the incident, Jay and Raghu tried to tell Avantika the truth. But she did not listen to anyone. She put in her resignation. Neel did as well. Raghu rejected both the applications.

Neel and Avantika parted ways. Avantika sent a divorce letter to Neel. But Neel did not sign it and Avantika did not ask for it.

Neel's suite, Muscat, Oman

Neel and Avantika were in Neel's suite. Neel narrated the complete incident to Avantika. She had tears in her eyes. She got up from the chair and hugged Neel. Neel too could not control his tears and hugged her tightly.

'I am sorry Avantika. I am really sorry . . .' said Neel.

'Just shut up. Don't say sorry. I love you,' said Avantika.

'I love you too, my dear wife.'

'Why didn't you tell me this earlier?'

'You did not give me a single chance!'

'Anyway, I am happy we are back together,' said Avantika and paused. She looked deep into Neel's eyes. Neel stared back at her. They came close and passionately kissed each other. Later, on the bed, they did not stop each other in any way and fell in love all over again. Their souls fell in love.

That night, Avantika and Neel were together in Neel's suite. Jay was unaware about their reunion. Neel got up early in the morning, went, and glanced out of the window. The sun was about to rise.

He opened the drawer where he had kept the map and the piece of paper. He unfolded the map and stared at it. He counted the markings on the map. They were eight. Then he counted the letters of the unknown word, they too were eight.

He took his phone and called Jay, 'Jay, get up! I've found a clue!'

'What? I am still sleeping! I will come when I am ready,' he said and ended the call.

After the call, Neel kept the map and the paper aside. He went to Avantika and ran his fingers through her hair. She opened her eyes gradually.

'Good morning, my dear husband . . .' she said.

'Good morning. I found something!'

'What?'

'Well, I had found a piece of paper and a map yesterday at the site of the murder,' Neel said and explained everything to her.

After getting ready, Jay came into Neel's suite. He was shocked to see Avantika there.

'What the hell! You both were together? Am I dreaming?'

'No, we sorted it out! Now we are together again,' replied Avantika smiling.

'Congratulations! That's great.'

'Thank you!' they said in unison and laughed.

Suddenly, Neel's phone rang. It was the Omani officer.

'Sir, can you come to the office? Shankar has confessed,' said the officer.

'Yes, we will be there as soon as we can,' said Neel and gestured to the two to get ready.

The officer was already in the office waiting for them when they reached. They went into the cabin and he told them to have a seat.

'Shankar has confessed that he killed Shivam. Shivam and Shankar murdered Akash Gupta and had managed to make it look like a suicide,' said the officer.

'What? Shivam and Shankar killed Akash? But why?' said Avantika.

'Exactly, I knew that!' said Neel.

'Well, it is a long story. Shivam, Shankar and Akash were working together on a film. Akash was having an affair with an actress. He was making a film on Vasco da Gama. He needed Shivam's help because Shivam had already made a film on Vasco da Gama earlier. The storyline was that some south Indian person tries to kill Da Gama but he fails. And now, the story of the film Akash was trying to make was totally opposite to the film made earlier.'

'But that can't be the reason to murder someone?' asked Avantika.

'Shivam had a negative image of Da Gama in his mind. One incident that took place in Da Gama's life destroyed his image. It is said that Da Gama once killed four hundred people to acquire a ship. The ship was sailing from India to Mecca. Da Gama killed all the passengers and captured the ship. And that was the incident that got stuck in his mind. The incident is called the Pilgrim Ship incident. Shivam had made a film on the same story. If Akash would direct a film in favour of Da Gama, then it would create a wrong image of Da Gama in people's hearts, thought Shivam. Therefore, he blackmailed Akash that he would inform his wife about his affair. He would call him from an unknown number and not reveal his real identity. Akash got frightened. That day, Shivam told Akash to get rid of everyone in the house. Akash did what Shivam told him to do. Shivam and Shankar took Akash from his home and took him to some place out of the city. They threatened him and then took him back. They tied a rope and forced him to hang himself.'

'But what about Akash's wife?' said Neel.

'Shivam had forced him to tell his wife to visit her parents. Akash's wife did as Akash told her to do.'

'Fine, so that was all planned beautifully!' exclaimed Avantika.

'It does not end there.'

'There's more?' asked Avantika.

'The artefacts! Shankar and Shivam hired a local team in Oman and stole the artefacts. When they came to know that the artefacts belonged to Vasco da Gama, Shivam decided to steal them. Shankar helped Shivam. They stole the items but when Shivam did not give him his share, Shankar stabbed Shivam.'

'Where are the artefacts now?' asked Neel.

'Shankar heard dying Shivam say that the artefacts had been hidden in different places across the world. But no one knows the exact location of the artefacts.'

'But why did he do that?' asked Neel.

'For fame! He had to make a name in history.'

'Well, I found a piece of paper and a world map from the room where Shivam was murdered. The paper has a mysterious word written on it and the map is marked with symbols,' said Neel and took them out from his pocket.

'Sir, you should not have hidden evidence from us, and I am sure you know that. Strict action can be taken against you for this. But for now, I am glad we have something. They'll help us to find the artefacts,' said the officer.

'The map has eight markings on it and the word has eight letters,' said Neel and handed it to the officer. The Omani officer unfolded the paper.

MMCCMMCL

Then he unfolded the map and studied it. It had eight markings alright.

'There are eight markings as you said: on Portugal, Egypt and Cape Town; there are two in south India and Kenya and one in Mozambique,' said the officer.

'What are these markings?' asked Avantika.

'I can't understand. There are two small circles made on south India, there are two symbols on Kenya, one is oval and the second is a circle in a circle, there is a dot in a circle on Mozambique, there is a triangle on Cape Town; there is a rectangle on Egypt... I think it's on Cairo. And there is a triangle in a circle on Portugal, and it must be on Lisbon,' said the officer.

'Can I get the photos of the missing artefacts? I think Shivam has made the symbols according to the missing artefacts,' said Neel.

'But how can we know where the artefacts will be kept? The cities are not small places to find anything.'

'We can get that from history. We will have to find the relation of these cities with Vasco da Gama's voyage,' said Neel.

'There must be something relating to Da Gama in these cities,' said Avantika.

'Here are the photographs!' said the Omani officer and handed over the photos to Neel.

Neel observed them carefully. The bell, the coins, the barrel, the disc, the sheave, the beads, and the canon ball.

'I think the circles made on South India are for the coins, the rectangle for the barrel, a triangle for the bell, the oval for beads. There are three more circles: for the canon ball, the sheave and the disc,' said Neel.

'Perfect!' exclaimed the officer.

'What about the word on the paper? It also has eight letters,' said Avantika.

'It may be the initials of the cities or of the artefacts,' said the Omani officer.

'It's of the cities! 'L' is for Lisbon; the triangle in the circle is exactly done on Lisbon. 'C' for Cairo, the rectangle for the barrel is on Cairo. In Mozambique, the dot in a circle is on Maputo, the capital of Mozambique. One city in India must be Calicut; everyone knows Vasco da Gama landed there. There are two symbols on Kenya; we will have to find out those cities from the map. The other 'C' is for Cape Town; the triangle, the bell must be in Cape Town!' said Neel in excitement.

'Check the route of Vasco da Gama when he sailed to India,' said Avantika.

'Exactly, he stayed in Kenya at two places; one is Mombasa and other Malindi. He also stayed near the coast in Maputo in Mozambique,' said Neel researching it on the internet.

'So the cities are Calicut, Maputo, Malindi, Mombasa, Cape Town, Lisbon and Cairo. One city in South India is missing,' said the Omani Officer.

'We need to find a city with initial 'M', located in South India and related to Vasco da Gama,' said Neel and started browsing the internet and the map.

'Now what about the symbols and the artefacts?' asked the officer.

'The circle in a circle can be of the disc or the sheave, and the dot in a circle for the canon ball. There is a triangle in a circle, I think it's for the disc,' said Avantika.

'Got it! It's Madayi, a small village in Kerala. The Pilgrim Ship incident took place in Madayi,' said Neel.

'Two coins in India – one in Madayi and one in Calicut. The bell in Cape Town, the barrel in Cairo, the sheave in Malindi, the beads in Mombasa, the canon ball in Maputo and the disc in Lisbon,' said Avantika.

'But still we don't know the exact location of the artefacts! We have got only the name of the cities!' said Neel. 'I will speak with Raghu and give him an update,' said Neel and went out to call him.

'Neel, if you are sure about the eight artefacts in the eight cities, then you can go and find them yourself! The Indian government and the Omani government will support you in this mission. I will have a word with the Omani, and you will get all support from them as well,' said Raghu.

'But sir, that's going to be a long tour!'

'So what? We need the artefacts! You have your wife with you. You will get time to win her back.'

'Well, sir, we sorted out the matter yesterday.'

'Wonderful! Then go for a trip together' said Raghu.

When Neel finished his conversation with Raghu, he saw Avantika and Jay behind him, discussing something. He went towards them.

'What did he say?' asked Avantika.

'He told us to go and find the artefacts in the eight cities,' said Neel.

'What! It is not going to be an easy task,' exclaimed Avantika.

'But we have to go and find them!'

'It's not that easy, Neel. We only know the names of the cities!' said Avantika.

'We can find the exact location by studying the history related to the objects, I am sure,' said Neel.

'If it is an adventure, then I am coming,' said Jay.

'I don't know about an adventure, but we will of course enjoy the hunt,' Neel said.'

'I will have to think about it,' said Avantika.

'I hope you will accompany us in the beautiful artefact-hunt,' said Jay.

Avantika had faith in Neel's deductions, but she wanted some relief from the consuming cases. After clearing the misunderstanding with Neel, she was now looking forward to a healthy relation with him. She wanted to live with Neel. She wanted to recover the lost time with her husband.

The night fell with one mystery solved. But the three had a long journey to go on to find the missing artefacts. Neel sighed and got into bed. He knew the real challenge was to locate the artefacts in the eight cities. But he felt more confident and complete with his wife coming back into his life.

I am ready to find all the artefacts in one go, if Avantika is next to me and loving me every minute.

A smile appeared on his face when he closed his eyes and saw Avantika's beautiful smile. His vision was disturbed by the doorbell. He got up and opened to door only to see Avantika standing at the door with her luggage.

'What happened? Is everything fine?' Neel asked.

'Yes, I am just shifting my bags here,' said Avantika and walked into the room.

'Shifting? I didn't get it.'

'Yes, shifting! Do you have any problem sharing your room and your bed with your wife?' said Avantika and placed her bags inside the room.

'No, absolutely not!' said Neel and smiled.

He added, 'But I am not comfortable sharing my bed. You see, the bed is not so large and you take a lot of space. I literally get thrown out of the bed. So why should I compromise my sleep or sleep on the corner of the bed, that too on one side, not knowing at which moment I will have a meeting with the floor?' He was looking right into her eyes.

'So who told you to clear the misunderstanding between us? Now if you have done it, you will have to face the consequences,' said Avantika and put her hands on Neel's shoulders.

'But we hadn't agreed to share the bed.'

'Fine, then no problem! You can have a sound sleep on the sofa,' said Avantika in a low voice. They were quite close to each other by now. Only a few centimeters separated them.

'No, I think I can adjust,' protested Neel.

'No! I can't see you uncomfortable. You don't have to adjust. You can sleep peacefully on the sofa.'

'Then why did you shift to my room? To let me sleep on the sofa?'

'You are uncomfortable with me, but I have no problem with you,' Avantika played along.

'Then why don't we do one thing?'

'What? Now don't tell me to shift to another suite.'

'No, but what if I sleep on the bed and you on the sofa?' said Neel and smiled.

'You ...' Avantika protested and hit him with a pillow. Neel caught the pillow and threw it back at her.

'Fine, now let's go for dinner. Jay will be waiting for us,' said Avantika.

'Let's give him a surprise.'

'About what?'

'Let's go together to his suite and invite him for dinner.'

'Let's do it. Get ready!'

After getting ready, Neel and Avantika went to Jay's suite. Avantika knocked the door. Neel softly touched Avantika's fingers. Avantika noticed the touch and held Neel's hand. Suddenly the door opened and Jay saw them both holding hands.

'Oh... So you are finally together!' Jay exclaimed with joy.

'Yes... Finally,' replied Avantika.

'Let's go for dinner,' commented Neel.

'Ah! Else why would you waste your time with me?' said Jay.

'Exactly!' Neel said casually.

'Shut up,' interrupted Avantika. 'C'mon, let's move!'

After enjoying the Omani food, Jay went towards his suite. Neel and Avantika went into Neel's suite.

'So what have you decided?' asked Avantika.

'About what?'

'Sofa or bed?'

'Bed, and you on the sofa.'

'Shut up!'

'Avantika.'

'What? I am not going to sleep on the sofa.'

'It's not that. I feel really happy that we are back.'

'Yes. I knew we would be together. And here we are in an unknown place in an unknown situation, far away from our country, solving an unknown case,' said Avantika and went close to Neel.

'Why is it that everyone needs a partner? When I was away from you, I missed you. I learnt that I really loved you. Why is it that we understand the importance of our loved ones when they are away from us?' Neel said softly.

'I don't know about the philosophy, but what I only know is I love you. And I am with you.'

'You are just wonderful!' said Neel and hugged Avantika.

After the emotional scene, they retired to bed. Of course, both of them shared the bed and made love like two newlyweds.

'The distance which takes the loved ones away from us, also gets us closer after the darkness vanishes. This is the beautiful law of love. As the earth is round, one reaches the same place after circumnavigating the globe. The same applies for love. The beautiful phases of love – the ups and downs, the enormous journey of two hearts – are to be enjoyed in the adventure of life,' Neel said to himself.

The next morning, Avantika woke up early. She opened her eyes as the rays of sunshine made its way into the room to fill it with golden light. She looked at Neel. He was still sleeping. She kissed him on his forehead and got up from the bed. Then, she moved towards the window. The morning traffic on the road was clearly visible from the window. The beautiful capital city of Oman glowed in the sunshine. The upcoming day was reserved for exploring the city.

'This is the itinerary: first the Sultan Qaboos Grand Mosque, then the Al Ameen Mosque, then Bait Al Zubair and then the National Museum,' said Neel.

'What do you know about these places?' asked Avantika.

'We are here to learn about them. I have a map and I know the route,' said Neel and paused as he received a call from the cab driver. He told Jay to check out the cab.

The cab was waiting outside the hotel when Jay went to check. He called Neel and told him to get ready and join him. Within a few minutes, Neel and Avantika came over walking hand in hand. That brought a smile on Jay's excited face.

'C'mon, let us go,' said Avantika.

'Ya, let us go. I have been waiting for you guys for ages,' replied Jay.

'So rude! We came down within five minutes after you called Neel,' said Avantika.

'Fine, let's go! I am sure you will be comfortable in the front seat,' said Neel and smiled.

'Yes, of course. Now I am jealous of you Avantika. Alas! I don't have a wife or a girlfriend,' said Jay.

They walked towards the cab. Jay went and sat on the front seat. Avantika and Neel sat on the backseat. Jay told the driver to head towards the Sultan Qaboos Grand Mosque.

'Why don't you get married after our historical treasure hunt? Everyone needs a partner!' said Avantika.

'So you have agreed to join us in the treasure hunt? Great! It will be fun. It will be our longest trip ever,' said Jay.

'I don't think it will be fun,' interrupted Neel.

'Whatever! But it can be fun when we all are together.'

'I think we were talking about your marriage,' interrupted Avantika.

'Yes, do you have a sister?' asked Jay.

'No,' replied Avantika making a face.

'Fine, then you find me a perfect partner.'

'No, I can't.'

'Leave it! I shall find you a bride,' said Neel.

'No, thank you. I am fine single,' said Jay.

Avantika saw Neel's hand and moved her hand close to it. She rolled her fingers on Neel's hand. That caught Neel's attention. He saw Avantika and understood her silent words, 'I am happy we are together.' Avantika gave a beautiful smile and Neel reciprocated.

They reached their first destination, the Sultan Qaboos Grand Mosque. The beautiful architecture was clearly visible from a distance. The tall entrances, the large pillars, the dome of the mosque and the walls were shining white in the glowing sunlight.

'Wow! Such a big mosque!' exclaimed Avantika.

'Yeah, it's beautiful. It is the largest mosque in Oman,' said Neel.

They entered the mosque only to be stunned to see the beauty of the interiors. The beauty of the large fountains, the tall pillars, the large doors and entrances, the large dome, the reflecting tiles and the white sandstone were hard to describe. There were minute as well as large carvings in the sandstone. It was full of people admiring its beauty.

'Do you know that the carpet in the praying hall is the second largest hand-woven carpet in the world? It took four years to complete the carpet. It has 1.7 billion knots and its weight is 21 tons. I am eagerly waiting to see it,' said Neel.

'Wow, that sounds so fascinating. Let's go in,' said Avantika.

They went inside the mosque admiring the minute details on the sandstone. The large praying hall was shining with the gold plated chandelier in the middle.

'The chandelier is made up of sixty thousand crystals. It is lit with more than one thousand halogen bulbs. And it is the second largest in the world. The entire mosque is built in the style of Islamic Indian art,' whispered Neel.

'How do you know all this?' asked Avantika.

'I researched yesterday,' replied Neel.

'It's beautiful,' whispered Avantika.

After staying a while in the praying hall, they went out. They explored the gardens in the vicinity and took some photos.

'So at last, picture perfect. You look wonderful together!' said Jay when he took their photo.

They then headed to their next destination, the Al Ameen mosque. Avantika looked at the pictures that Jay had taken. She chose one picture of Neel and her together, and set it as the wallpaper of her phone screen. She showed it to Neel and smiled.

'Beautiful, right? I've got a chance to set our picture as my phone wallpaper after a long time,' said Avantika.

'It's beautiful,' said Neel.

Soon they reached their destination. The mosque was shining white in the daylight. It was constructed with marble and sandstone. The beautiful architecture and carvings gained Jay's undivided attention as he got busy taking photos.

'Do you know that the floors are all air-conditioned? When we step on the floor even when it's really hot, they will be cool. Isn't it crazy,' said Jay.

'Wow! That's great. I was wondering how the floors were so cool,' said Avantika.

'I guess you already knew that,' Jay said to Neel.

'It was the same at the Sultan Qaboos Grand mosque. I think you didn't notice,' said Neel.

The doors and the windows were huge. The brown wooden doors added to the beauty of the white shining mosque. The upper side of the doors had something written in Arabic.

They moved inside the mosque. It was smaller compared to the Grand mosque. The three chandeliers were emitting light in beautiful colours. The carpets were similar to the ones at the Grand mosque but smaller in size. The dome and the two pillars were in the style of classical architecture.

'It feels so calm and quiet here,' said Avantika.

'The silence and the lights say it all. And the refreshing whiteness of the mosque is extraordinary,' said Neel.

Jay was silent and enjoying the silence. After exploring all the parts of the mosque, they left for the Bait Al Zubair museum.

Neel and Avantika occupied the back seat. Avantika was happy. She constantly stared at Neel. As they were not alone, Neel tried to postpone the 'looking into the eyes session'. Jay caught Avantika staring at Neel. He also saw how Neel was trying to fight the situation.

'Do you guys want to see more places? We can go back to the hotel if you are tired. Because if we go now to the next museum, we will be late,' said Jay. He knew how much Avantika wanted a moment with Neel alone.

'No, it's fine. We will go to the museum. I want to see more of Oman,' said Avantika and looked at Neel. 'With you,' she added.

Neel smiled and so did Jay. They reached the fort like domed entrance of the museum soon.

'It feels like we are on a film set,' said Jay.

They proceeded inside. There were several rooms on separate floors of different departments. It had male and female attire rooms in Omani style. The classic old jewelry room had the beautiful female ornaments preserved. The swords, stamps, coins and medals of the old times were also kept in the safe house. It also contained antique maps and prints that had been printed long back. The main room to visit was the manuscript room, which had old and rare books displayed. The next room was the one that housed the 'khanjar', the dagger that the men used. The everyday attire of the Sultan and the people included a dagger. The ornamented dagger of the Sultan's private collection was breathtakingly beautiful.

'What a collection!' said Avantika.

'Yes. All the items were beautiful. History comes alive in front of the eyes,' said Neel.

'Where do we go next?' asked Avantika.

'The national museum. We can get all the information on the history of Oman,' said Neel.

'Fine then, let's go,' said Avantika.

The national museum of Oman reflects the cultural heritage of Oman from about two million years ago. It has fourteen galleries with over five thousand objects. It is a treasure trove for any lover of history interested in learning about the cultural and geographical history of Oman, including its deep relation with Islam, its arms, armor, civilization, currency and heritage.

After the extraordinary visit, the three went back to the hotel. As informed by the Indian Embassy, they had an early morning flight to Lisbon.

When in the hotel room, Neel threw his jacket on the bed. Avantika retired to the bed. 'It was a nice trip!' she said, staring at Neel.

Neel sat on the sofa and was thinking of the next trip to Lisbon. He was wondering how they were going to come across a clue to lead them to the artefact in the city. Avantika got up from the bed and sat beside him. She put her head softly on Neel's shoulder.

'What are you thinking dear?' she asked.

'No, nothing!'

'Then come to the bed. I want you by my side when I get lost in my dreams. I want to have you by my side when I get up in the morning.'

'Oh! So you are still in the mode.'

'Of course, but you have lost your romance mode for sure.'

'No, it's not that.'

'Then what is it? We had such a beautiful day. But you were so serious. I know you are concerned about the case. But don't worry. We will figure it out together and everything will be fine. We will surely find the artefacts. I know you can and you will.'

'Yes, thanks. But don't you think that since the sun has gone down we should now get into bed and get lost in each other?'

'Sorry officer, but I was saying the same thing a while ago. And now you have lost the chance. Now you will have to earn it.'

'So what can I do to earn the chance to have you by my side when I wake up in the morning?'

'Well, think hard.'

'A cup of coffee?'

'It can do. But I think it's not enough.'

'You mean a cup of coffee with me isn't enough? Should I call Jay then?'

'Shut up and get into bed!' said Avantika and got up.

'What about coffee? You don't want a cup?'

'I want you! And you are so dumb!'

Neel smiled and so did Avantika. It was good to be back to their old selves. They went to bed and made love before falling into a long blissful sleep.

Neel got up in the middle of the night. He got up and drank some water. He then took out the map with the markings. After glancing at it for a while, he kept it aside.

'I need to find all the monuments and things related to Vasco da Gama in Lisbon,' he said to himself.

He then went back to bed.

The morning alarm rang at five. Avantika got up and switched it off. She glanced at Neel. He was half-asleep. She rolled her fingers on his eyes down to his lips. Neel seemed to like it. He raised his hand and did the same to her. She kissed his fingers.

'Good morning darling. It's time to get up. We have a flight to catch,' said Avantika.

'Yes, I know. I love you.'

'Yes, I know. I love you too.'

After getting ready, Neel, Avantika and Jay left the hotel and headed towards the airport. The airport was hardly half an hour away. Neel took a look at the beautiful city from the window of the car. The orange sun was rising and making its way for a brand new day. Neel had already started to miss Muscat. The beautiful city, which had given him his wife back.

He glanced at Avantika. She noticed his eyes. She smiled. Neel smiled back.

Lisbon, Portugal

'Welcome to Lisbon, sir,' the Indian diplomat said to Neel when they reached the airport.

'Thank you,' said Neel. Neel, Avantika, and Jay followed the Indian diplomat towards the exit. After settling down in the car, the diplomat started explaining the arrangements for the mission.

'Sir, we have made your arrangements in a safe house,' said the diplomat.

'Safe house? Last time I stayed at the hotel,' said Neel.

'Yes sir, but the Indian and the Portuguese governments do not want to publicize the mission. We don't want any leak or media attention,' replied the diplomat.

'As you deem fit,' said Neel.

They reached the safe house – a spacious 3BHK house.

'Sir, Rakesh sir will meet you tomorrow morning. Then you have an appointment with the police chief tomorrow. Rakesh sir will accompany you to the meeting. The Lisbon police will fully co-operate with you in locating the artefact,' said the diplomat.

'Thank you for your co-operation. I am happy we have a vast network of diplomats working all over the world. Working for our country in another nation is not easy I see. Thank you,' said Neel.

The diplomat smiled and left.

'If the government is the backbone of democracy, the diplomats are the backbone of the international image of the country,' said Neel to Avantika.

'Yes, it's true,' said Avantika in a professional tone.

'When I was here the last time, I was alone. When I went back to India, I met you. And now again, I am back here. But this time I am not alone. Feels great!' said Neel.

'It's always better with you around,' said Avantika and hugged Neel.

'Where is Jay? He hasn't troubled me for a while. Is he alright?' asked Neel.

'He is in his room. Must be getting ready for dinner.'

'Oh! So where do we have to go for dinner?'

'To a good romantic restaurant, I hope. Let's ask the driver outside.'

'That's Jay's work. He is a search engine.'

'Yes, I heard that,' interrupted Jay.

Neel and Avantika turned around in surprise. 'Don't worry, it'll be done. You both get ready,' said Jay with a bow.

Neel and Avantika, without uttering a word, went to their bedroom to freshen up. After getting ready, the three went to a restaurant which Jay had chosen.

'So what about the artefact? Where do we start the search?' asked Avantika after they made themselves comfortable in the restaurant.

'I think we should first find out about the monuments related to Vasco da Gama and then visit them and search for the artefacts,' said Neel.

'Only monuments?' asked Avantika.

'Then where else? Where will the artefact be?'

'I think we should explore all the things related to Vasco da Gama.'

'All things? Like?'

'The hotel, shopping complex, the Vasco da Gama Bridge.'

'Why would anyone hide the precious artefact in a shopping complex or a hotel or under a bridge?' asked Neel.

'Can't say! If one can steal the artefact, then he can keep it anywhere. I think we should search for it everywhere,' said Avantika.

'Fine. Let's see what the Portuguese are up to,' said Neel. 'I have made a complete list of all the monuments and places where the artefact may be hidden.'

'Well done! Can you tell me the names of the places?' said Avantika.

'I have selected six places – the Vasco da Gama Bridge, Vasco da Gama tower hotel, Vasco da Gama shopping centre, Jeronimos Monastery, where the tomb of Vasco da Gama is rested, then to Sines, where Vasco da Gama was born, there is a statue of Da Gama. The last one is Padrao dos Descobrimentos monument, where there is a statue of all the navigators of Portugal,' said Neel.

'Fantastic. Good job!' said Avantika.

The waiter arrived with the order. The Portuguese food which they were eagerly waiting to taste had arrived.

'So "fantastic" was for the food?' asked Neel.

'Yes, then what did you think it was for?' said Avantika and smiled. So did Jay.

'No, nothing! I think I was saying something.'

'The six places, right? Yes, I know them all!' said Avantika. 'I think we should have dinner first. I am hungry!'

'I am hungry too!' said Jay.

After having the much-awaited Portuguese dinner, the three made their way back to the house. The next day was to be long and they needed ample rest. Neel was visualizing everything about the case when Avantika suddenly appeared in his mind. When they reached the house, Neel made his way directly to the bedroom as he had unfinished work to do. He had to look over the map again and confirm the places with the symbols. He knew that the answers were present in the history of the place. The places he had listed were loosely related to the name of Da Gama or to Da Gama himself. Now the task for him was to seek permission from the Portuguese government to visit those places and search for the artefacts.

Avantika saw Neel sitting quietly lost in thoughts. She went to him and put her hands on his shoulders.

'What are you thinking dear?' she asked.

'Nothing, just thinking of tomorrow's work,' he said. He had been away from Avantika for a long time. The tiredness and the work pressure vanished automatically as soon as he felt her hands on his shoulders. He felt that everything would be all right if Avantika were by his side.

'Don't worry. We will find the first artefact soon. And then all the worries will fly away,' she said. And those were the words which Neel was waiting to hear. It brought satisfaction to Neel's heart. He gradually closed his eyes and let out a deep breath. Everything felt right with the world.

'C'mon, now get up and change. We need to rest so that we can give our best tomorrow,' said Avantika.

'I love you, my dear. You are my strength. Thank you,' said Neel holding her hand in his.

'The same applies to me, my dear. Don't copy my words, Neel,' said Avantika kissing his hands.

'Oh! Say it once again.'

'What? Don't copy my words?'

'Not that. Say my name.'

'Neel,' Avantika said softly.

'The way you say it, no one else can!'

'Oh really? What is special about that?'

'My name.'

'Shut up and get up,' said Avantika tapping him on his shoulder.

Neel got up and went to change. The night was dark, in stark contrast to the bright shining love of Neel and Avantika. They enjoyed the night's silence and went to bed.

The next morning, as scheduled, the Indian ambassador, Rakesh Sharma came to meet Neel at 10.

'Welcome back, Neel. Good to see you again and this time with your wife,' said Rakesh. Neel smiled and greeted him.

'So what about the missing artefacts? Where do you suspect it is hidden in Lisbon?' asked Rakesh.

'We have shortlisted six places. Five in Lisbon and the sixth one in Sines, the place where Vasco da Gama was born,' said Neel.

'Fine, we can go there. And which are the five places in Lisbon?'

'The bridge, there's a hotel, a shopping centre and two monuments.'

'There are cameras all over! We must first check out the video recordings of the places. And I think it's impossible to hide the artefact in a public place such as a shopping centre or hotel or the bridge.'

'Yes, but the monuments are also public places. There are lots of visitors there. How can one get there with the artefact and hide it there without being noticed?'

'What is the artefact?' Rakesh asked.

'It's a copper alloy disc.'

'Can I see a picture of it?'

'Yes,' said Neel and signalled to Jay to bring the photographs.

Rakesh saw the photos and said, 'I think it will be a tough job to hide such a disc. It can easily be seen.'

'Not when you have seen it once!' commented Neel.

'Yes, that's true. But I mean it can easily be recognized.'

'There are two options. The disc can either be buried or it can be placed in a space where it fits.'

'Okay, we will have all the places scanned. We will check all the CCTV footage and see if we can get something.'

'When do we have the meeting with the police chief?'

'We can go now. It's better to meet him in the morning rather than dealing with him when he gets really busy with the affairs of the country.'

'Fine then, let's go,' said Neel.

They went to meet the chief at his office. Neel explained the incidents and got his permission to explore the desired places. He was also told that the Portuguese government and the police would fully co-operate with them to find the artefact.

'I will talk with the authority of the shopping centre and we can get all the CCTV footage. The chief has also arranged for drone cameras to check the bridge,' said Rakesh when they came out of the office.

'That's great!' said Neel.

'We will also meet the Vasco da Gama hotel owner and seek the CCTV footage. The Indian Embassy has made all the arrangements for you to visit the two monuments and Sines. We will go to Sines tomorrow. It's a two-hour drive from Lisbon,' said Rakesh.

'Thank you Rakesh. It's been a great pleasure to work with you,' said Neel.

'It's our job Neel. Don't worry, we will find the artefact. We will not let the thieves harm India's international image,' said Rakesh walking to the car.

The Vasco da Gama Tower hotel is one of the tallest buildings in Lisbon. It is built over the Tagus River. After seeking permission to check the CCTV footage of the hotel, the four made their way towards the skyscraper. Along with them went a police car.

They reached the hotel and were amazed to see the huge architectural wonder. The hotel consists of two parts – the main hotel has twenty-two floors, and a tall huge structure to climb up and enjoy the view from. After having a look at the structure, they went in. The manager greeted them. He took them towards the camera room. Rakesh then told him to find out the history of the Indian guests in the hotel. But there were no Indian guests who had stayed in the hotel. They took copies of the footage and sent them to the police for investigation.

'Ask him if they had any problems with the CCTV cameras in the last few days,' said Neel to Rakesh. And Rakesh translated the question in Portuguese. Indian diplomats were usually fluent in the language of the country they are posted in.

'No, they haven't had any problems with the cameras. There has been no hacking in any of the systems either,' said Rakesh.

'I think we should ask the police to find out if there was information of hacking in any of the places we have shortlisted,' said Neel.

'Sure. I will contact them and let you know,' said Rakesh.

After examining the hotel thoroughly, they went back to the safe house. Rakesh dropped them and left. Dusk was about to fall. Neel went into the bedroom and studied the case files. Avantika went to freshen up and then sat next to Neel. She saw Neel studying the files. She silently stood up and made coffee for both. Then went and gave a cup to Neel. He was still busy with the files.

'Neel, have your coffee,' said Avantika.

'Just a minute sweetheart,' said Neel without shifting his eyes from the file.

'Done!' said Neel and kept the files aside.

'So, did you find anything?' asked Avantika.

'Nothing huge, but maybe a tiny clue that might help. C'mon, let's go out for a walk. I need fresh air,' said Neel and finished his coffee.

Avantika got up and gave her hand to Neel. He held her hand softly. He felt the warmth and the softness of her hand. It brought a smile and relief to his face. They went out to the lawn walking hand in hand.

'So, what have you found?' asked Avantika.

'I found a very important thing.'

'What is it? Did you find the perfect place where the artefact can be kept?'

'No, not that. It is more important than that.'

'What is it Neel?'

Neel held her hand tightly. Made her look at him. He then looked straight into her eyes and said, 'I have found out that your hands are really smooth. I never realized that earlier. I have found that you belong to me. The case made me forget it a hundred times, but the very next minute I realize I am with you. I have found that I am deeply in love with you and I found out that you too are in love with me.'

Avantika smiled and gave him a warm hug. It tightened every passing second. 'It is no need to say that I love you, but sometimes it becomes necessary,' said Avantika.

'I know, my dear wife.'

'Now will you tell me what you found out about the case?'

'Of course! But first you will have to release me,' said Neel, and Avantika released him.

'Fine, now tell me!'

'I think that if someone hates what history says and intends to change the perspective, then the person must make it popular among the people. To prove that history was wrong. And this can only be done by evil means.'

'Can't you just tell me in one sentence? Come to the point, Neel.'

'Yes, just pay attention to what I am saying.'

'Yes, Neel sir!'

'Therefore, in short, the artefacts will be kept only at historical places. And that too, popular historical places.'

'Yes, I know that.'

'You know everything! So you must know the place where the artefact is hidden.'

'Yes, according to me, the artefact hidden in Lisbon is a round copper alloy disc. The disc is dark brown in colour. So it needs to be hidden where it can't be found easily. Therefore, the historical place should also be similar in colour. And it should also have a place to hide a round disc.'

'Perfect! So first, we need to study the architecture of the monuments. And see where the disc can be hidden. And to do this work, we have Jay with us.'

'Where is he, by the way?'

'Must be sleeping. Let's see,' said Neel. They went into the house and entered Jay's bedroom. Neel had guessed correctly; he was having his evening nap. Neel went beside him and woke him up.

'What is it Neel? Why are you disturbing me?'

'You have some work to do now. You can sleep at night,' said Avantika.

'Now what?'

'Get up first and then I will tell you. Get up fast. Your coffee is waiting for you,' said Neel and moved out of the bedroom. Avantika went and made some coffee for Jay.

After a while, Jay came out of his bedroom into the living area. He saw a cup of coffee on the table. Neel and Avantika were sitting on the couch waiting for him.

'Why are you being so kind to me? What is it?' asked Jay.

'Nothing much. Have your coffee first,' said Neel.

'I will anyway do what you are going to tell me. There is no need for coffee. I am here to help you,' said Jay.

'Oh, so kind of you. Now listen. You will have to study the architecture of the monuments related to Vasco da Gama. Every small detail. And see where the rounded disc could be hidden easily. The monuments should be brown in colour, matching the disc, which is also brown. You also have the size of the disc. Now just find out where it can be hidden easily,' said Neel.

'I think I will need more coffee for this work,' said Jay rubbing his hands.

'Yes, you can have as much as you want. Just find the place,' said Neel.

Jay took the laptop and started searching for the monuments. He told Neel that he would need time. Neel sat beside and helped him with the list of monuments.

After a while, Neel got up and said, 'There are a lot of places. I don't think we can get it from here. We need to visit the place ourselves.'

'We have to go to Sines tomorrow, so let's start there,' said Avantika.

'Absolutely right!' said Jay.

'Okay then,' said Neel.

'Now let's get some food. I am hungry,' said Jay and kept the laptop aside.

Neel glanced at the watch. The time was 8:30 p.m. 'Let's have dinner,' said Neel. He told Jay to order the food from a restaurant. Jay was quick with that. They ate and they slept. The next day was going to be a long one, they knew.

Rakesh was waiting outside the safe house. Neel, Avantika and Jay were almost ready and grabbing the last minute stuff. Within a while, Neel went out of the house and greeted Rakesh.

'Good morning. I have asked the police to check all the CCTV recordings of the monuments,' said Rakesh.

'I hope we will get something in the cameras. It will be a direct proof of the robbery. Did you ask about hacking?' said Neel.

'No, they did not have any such problem. But yes, they had some minor issues with the cameras. But they said it was a regular problem.'

'I don't think the fault with the cameras is regular.'

'We will see to it when we get all the footage.'

'We need to concentrate on the monuments rather than hotels and shopping malls. It is easier to hide the artefact in the monuments,' Neel summed up.

Jay and Avantika came out of the house and the conversation ended. Jay was busy reading something on his phone. They got into the car and left for Sines.

The beautiful old city is located near the coast of the North Atlantic Ocean.

A police car followed them and in two hours, they had reached their destination – a small fort-like structure, which had a statue of Vasco da Gama with a small museum. Neel got out of the car. The hot sun was shining and reflecting its rays on the sea. He glanced at the endless waters of the ocean. He asked Rakesh about the statue. Rakesh took the three of them towards the statue. The fort had been constructed with stone, using white lime as mortar.

As they took a turn, they saw a dark brown statue. The name of Vasco da Gama was imprinted on the base of the statue. The statue was facing the huge sea in front. Neel examined the statue carefully. He could see no fault with it. His sharp eyes were looking for the first artefact all over the statue.

'I see no sign of the artefact here!' said Neel.

'May be we should search beneath the ground. The artefact may be buried down here,' said Avantika.

'But the ground is clear. There is no sign of any recent digging anywhere,' said Neel.

'Yes, the ground is covered with grass. And the statue is clean. I don't think the first artefact is here,' said Jay.

'Take photographs of the place. Don't leave any suspicious corner,' said Neel.

'Don't worry, Neel. I took a video,' said Jay.

'We need photographs too.'

'Yes boss. I am on it.'

'Good!'

After exploring the place and examining every corner of the statue, they went to the museum. The museum was small and didn't have anything that could be helpful, so they made their way back to Lisbon.

Rakesh had made all arrangements for them to visit the Vasco da Gama Bridge. The longest bridge in Europe, it is approximately seventeen kilometres long. It is rested on big columns with cables attached on one end of the bridge.

'We have placed two drone cameras on both sides of the bridge. It will give us the view from over the bridge,' said Rakesh when their car stopped at one end of the bridge.

Neel got out of the car and glanced over bridge. The bridge was spanning all over the Tagus River. The fading image of the other end of the bridge stood proof of its length.

'It would be better if we could gain access of the passengers list from the toll booths,' said Neel.

'The car numbers and the passengers are already recorded in the cameras. We will get the footage tomorrow,' replied Rakesh.

'We can also get information from the taxi owners or their unions,' said Jay putting in his two cents.

'Let's go! We will drive along the bridge,' said Rakesh. Everyone got into the car. Neel kept his eyes stuck on the window and told Jay to do the same. But they could see nothing unusual. Disappointed, they returned to the safe house.

'Thanks Rakesh for your tremendous contribution in the case,' said Neel when Rakesh was leaving.

'No, it is my job. By the way, the police department told me that they visited and checked the shopping mall,' said Rakesh.

'And?'

'They found nothing.'

'No problem. We still have tomorrow.'

'Yes, tomorrow we have to visit a monument and an old church. The tomb of Vasco da Gama is in the church.'

'Let's see what we can find tomorrow.'

Rakesh left and Neel got back into the house. As soon as he entered the house, Avantika told him that she had found something. Jay and Avantika were busy looking for something on the laptop.

'I am pretty sure the artefact is here!' said Avantika looking for something on the internet.

'Where?' asked Neel.

'The church – Jeronimos Monastery. The place where the tomb of Vasco da Gama is laid. A figure of Vasco da Gama is carved over the tomb. The tomb has carvings on it. It is easy to hide the circular disc there,' said Avantika.

'The place has cameras everywhere,' said Neel.

'Yes, and no one can enter the place without passing the checking post,' said Jay.

'The disc is made of copper and no one would ever know about the disc. No one would check the disc,' protested Avantika.

'But we have cameras there Jay. How can anyone pass the cameras and hide the disc near the tomb?' said Neel.

'Let's go and find out tomorrow!' exclaimed Avantika.

'Fine,' said Neel.

'You need to call Raghu,' said Avantika. 'I got a message from him.'

Neel took out his phone and called Raghu. He told him about the places he had visited. He also told him that he had found nothing. Raghu told him to visit as many places as he needed to.

'We have shifted Shankar to India. He is in jail in Mumbai,' said Raghu.

'Does he know the places? Does he know anything at all?' asked Neel.

'No, he doesn't. We tried our best, but he is blank.'

'Fine, we will visit two monuments tomorrow. Let's see what we find.'

'Do let me know what happens'

After the call, Neel kept the phone aside and sat on a couch. Avantika sat down next to him.

'God knows when we will find the disc. I am not even sure if we will be able to find it at all. We are running all over only on the basis of the map,' said Neel.

'We will find it tomorrow. I don't know how and where, but I think we will. We will not waste this trip, trust me,' said Avantika and patted him on his shoulder. It clearly meant that no matter what, she was with him. She trusted Neel and she was ready to face anything with Neel.

The next day, the three along with Rakesh reached the Jeronimos Monastery located near the Tagus River. The old building is a world heritage site. It is one of the best examples of Portuguese architecture. The huge building is teeming with visitors every day. It has two museums on the west wing. The beautiful design of the arches is something for the eyes to behold.

Neel asked Rakesh to lead him straight towards the tomb. The police surrounded the place and sealed it to stop the visitors from entering. A huge portrait hung up on the other side of the tomb.

The carved figure of Vasco da Gama lay on the tomb. The tomb was covered with carvings on all sides. Some quotes were carved on the tomb in Portuguese. Neel went closer and took a brief look at the tomb. He saw a carving of a ship on one side of the tomb.

Jay and Avantika glanced at every detail on the tomb. Rakesh saw a camera recording the area. He told the police to get the footage of the camera.

'It's not here,' said Avantika.

'I know. Why would anyone risk keeping the disc here? Can't you see the camera is watching this tomb?' said Neel.

'It's impossible to hide the disc here,' said Rakesh.

'Rakesh, can you please tell the police to check the entire place? The architecture is most suitable for the disc to be hidden. We can't take a chance,' said Neel and moved out of the place.

'Of course!' said Rakesh and followed Neel.

'Where is the next destination?' asked Neel.

'Right in front of us. The monument besides the river,' said Rakesh.

'What's its name? I forgot its name,' said Neel.

'Padrao dos Descobrimentos. The monument is located where ships used to depart for trade and exploration at that time. It was built to celebrate the age of exploration in the 15th and 16th century. It has statues of explorers, artists, scientists and missionaries. The first one right in front is of Henry the navigator,' said Rakesh.

'And Vasco da Gama?' asked Neel.

'His statue is on the eastern side that is facing the river. His statue is the third one.'

'Let's go,' said Neel as he nodded at the information.

They walked towards the monument. Neel could see the tall monument from a distance. The monument had statues of the personalities in a line and on both the sides. Neel went close to it. Down on the floor he saw a huge compass with a world map on it. It was made of limestone. The map had routes marked on it with all the information of the Portuguese explorers. Neel had a feeling that he would get his first artefact here.

He moved straight to the eastern side of the monument. He was walking fast in excitement. Jay and Avantika were studying the monument with great care. Their eyes were continuously searching out for the disc.

Neel got closer to the monument. With a stroke, he scanned the eastern side of the monument. It was still morning. The bright sunlight was falling on the monument, making it easy for Neel to scan it. He remembered Rakesh's words. The third statue was that of Vasco da Gama.

At last, he stood in front of the statue. He scanned the statue with his detective eyes. The statue was holding a sword in his left hand. His eyes fell on the sword. Right above the sword, he saw a circular plate balanced. The plate was placed near the sword. It was clearly visible that it didn't belong there.

A sense of satisfaction rolled down his body. 'And there I find you!' he said to himself. Jay and Avantika came and stood beside Neel. Neel showed them the disc pointing with his hand.

'Oh my god! We found it. We will need something to go up there,' said Avantika.

Rakesh also joined them and said, 'Don't worry! The police will bring it down.'

They went back to their house jubilantly. The police took the artefact for further investigation. According to the police, they would return the artefact to where it came from – Oman.

'So the question is how was it brought here?' said Avantika. The four of them were at the safe house now.

'Beside the monument, there was a harbour. I think it would have come by sea. But the question is how could anyone go up there on the monument and put the disc there!' said Neel.

'The police had issues with the camera during the nights. They were not sure about the hacking, but they definitely had a problem with the cameras. I think that must have been case. And so, no one saw the artefact being placed on the statue,' said Rakesh.

'A well planned thing! I think there are more people involved in this robbery,' said Avantika.

'But why would anyone keep the artefacts hidden in monuments? And that too in eight different cities and countries,' said Neel.

'It's because of that mad Shivam and Shankar. I think they both had lost their minds completely!' said Jay.

'They are not mad. A mad person cannot execute such a perfect plan. I think a lot more is to come,' said Neel.

'It's only that Shivam hates Vasco da Gama because of the Pilgrim Ship incident. And now, he has got the chance to threaten us! He is doing it only for the sake of altering history. He lost his life. He killed Akash and now he has got us,' said Jay.

'To go to such lengths only to alter history?' asked Rakesh.

'I have known many people who are crazy about history. They love history and they hate history! If they love it, then they tell stories of it. If they hate it, then they try to change it. But history cannot be changed. So they try to show the people what was wrong,' said Jay.

'Nice speech. But still, I think that there is more to come,' said Neel.

'Thanks for the compliment,' said Jay.

'Let's not argue and be ready to face everything that comes our way,' said Avantika.

That night, Neel sat alone in the bedroom brooding over the scenes. Avantika came in and placed her hand over his head. That brought relief to Neel's heart.

'We found it dear! Now stop brooding,' said Avantika softly.

'Yes dear. Thank you for being by my side.'

'Now what? What is our next destination?'

'Cairo.'

Neel called Raghu and informed him about the discovery. He told Neel he would make the arrangements in Cairo.

The next morning, Neel got up with a start. As soon as he opened his eyes, he saw Jay in front of him.

'You need to see this,' said Jay in an urgent manner.

'What is wrong?' asked Neel.

'Just come with me,' said Jay and took him in the living room. Avantika was already there. The TV was on. Avantika was watching the news with rapt attention.

'It's in the news Neel! Someone leaked it to the media,' said Avantika.

'What? I thought it was a secret mission!' said Neel. 'I need to call Rakesh.'

Neel took his phone and called Rakesh. He already knew about it.

'We took utmost care. But when we visited the monuments yesterday with the police force, someone leaked it to the media. I had a word with the government. Within a while, the news will be stopped from being broadcasted,' said Rakesh.

'If the case gets media attention and if it becomes public, then it will be difficult to find the other artefacts,' said Neel.

'Don't worry Neel, I will personally see that it is hushed up.'

As promised by Rakesh, the news was stopped from being shown. But Neel was worried that people had already come to know of the discovery of the artefact. And he knew people like to spread stories, and every time with exaggeration.

'It's time to go now!' said Neel.

'Yes, it's time!'

'So which city is waiting for us?' asked Jay.

'The city of the pyramids!'

Cairo, Egypt

The historic city of the pyramids, the capital of Egypt, Cairo, is one of the oldest cities in the world. The beautiful city is located along the delta region of the river Nile.

The sun was setting and the moon was slightly visible. The huge city was glowing with lights. Neel, Avantika and Jay landed in Cairo. An Indian diplomat was waiting for their arrival at the airport. He met the three and took them towards the parking lot. Then they made their way to the safe house which they were going to use for this mission.

The diplomat asked Neel about the places he wanted to visit so that he could make adequate arrangements. Neel told him that he would inform him after researching a bit. The diplomat dropped them to the safe house and left. Neel told Avantika and Jay to finalize the destinations they wanted to visit.

'I think we should visit old Cairo city. Most of the famous churches and the museums are located there,' said Avantika.

'But I don't think the second artefact would be there. What is the symbol in the map? What is the artefact in Cairo?' asked Neel.

'It's a barrel! A pipe like structure around twenty-five centimeters in length. It's not that large and pretty easy to hide,' said Avantika.

'Which places do you think it will be in?' asked Neel.

'First is the Coptic museum – the largest museum of Egyptian Christian artefacts in the world. The second and the third are the famous Babylon fortress and the hanging church,' said Avantika.

'So you think it would be either in the church or in a museum?' asked Neel.

'I am not sure, but we have to look at both the places. The three monuments are very close to each other.'

'Cairo is also famous for Islamic architecture and mosques,' said Neel.

'Yes, I still have to read up about them. Tomorrow we will visit the three places and then decide the rest of the places. I need some time for that.'

'Fine, now let's go and get some sleep! My dear wife, can you please join me in my dreams?' Neel asked Avantika.

Avantika smiled and said, 'Yes, my dear husband.'

Jay had his eyes fixed on the laptop. But his ears were focused on Neel's words. He gave a naughty smile before concentrating on his work again.

Neel and Avantika went into the bedroom and settled on the bed.

'Mister husband! Don't you think you should help Jay find the places?'

'No, not today! I am tired and I need sleep. And I want you by my side.'

'No way! I am going to help Jay. You get your sleep. I am not sleepy. I will join you later.'

'Of course not! Join me now or join me never.'

'You can sleep without me. You did for a year, right?'

'What do you think? Can you stay forever? Without me?'

'When I was away, I kept on telling myself that I have to be away from you forever. But I don't know why, somewhere in the heart, I felt we'd get back together.'

'I too want to confess!' said Neel. He moved close to Avantika. They were lying on the bed looking into each other's eyes.

'So what are you waiting for?' said Avantika softly.

'When you were away, I was alone in our house. The walls, the doors, and the windows seemed to be depressed without you. Whenever I used to be home, I felt a void. I felt I was wrong. I felt like quitting my job. I was about to give away everything that I had. But thanks to Jay, he supported me and stopped me every time when I went crazy. Life without you is crazy! It's hopeless. I can't express it in words, but I was dying,' said Neel.

'I can't wait for us to get home. We will have a wonderful holiday after this mission.'

'Yes, I am eagerly waiting for the time to come. No matter where we are, but we always love our own home.'

'I had never imagined this half of the world trip with you. I am so happy!'

'We've found only one of the eight artefacts. Seven more are to be located. It is not that easy,' said Neel. 'But now when you are with me, I am ready for anything!'

●

The Coptic Museum had been built in 1908. The museum was built to store Coptic art and was the largest museum of Coptic antiques. Neel, Avantika, Jay and the Indian diplomat went to the museum the next morning. Neel asked the police to check the footage of the cameras.

They had a look around the museum. The artefacts preserved there were precious. After having a look at the artefacts and the antiques, they moved towards the Hanging Church.

Neel thought it was impossible for anyone to hide the artefacts in a church or in a museum. He asked the police to check the footage of the famous churches and mosques.

He then asked the Indian diplomat to return to the safe house. It was going to be of no use visiting random monuments. They had to have a lead.

Jay said he needed more time to shortlist places related to Vasco da Gama in any way.

They reached the safe house and Jay got down to his work of finding a clue. Hours passed, but he did not find any.

'We have to read up more history,' said Neel.

'We need to know more about the Pilgrim Ship incident,' said Avantika.

'Vasco da Gama killed four hundred people to acquire a ship! The ship was heading to Mecca,' said Jay.

'Have we got an artefact placed in Mecca?' asked Avantika.

'No, we have no mark on Mecca on the map,' said Neel.

'The place where the pilgrim ship incident took place?' said Avantika.

'Madayi! We have a marking there on the map,' interrupted Jay.

'Vasco da Gama acquired the ship. And whose ship was it?' asked Neel.

'Let me find out,' said Jay. After a while, he exclaimed, 'I found it! It is here in Cairo.'

'Which place?' asked Avantika impatiently.

'The ship belonged to the Sultan of Egypt, Al-Ashraf Qansuh al-Ghawri.'

'So what's here in Cairo?' asked Neel.

'The Sultan Al-Ghuri Complex! The mosque, tomb and madrasa are located in this complex here in Cairo. The next artefact is definitely hidden there,' said Jay.

'Tell the diplomat and tell the police to check cameras. And get ready! We are going to the mosque right now,' exclaimed Neel.

The monument is located in old Cairo. It has sections on both sides of the road. A common roof joins both the sides and covers the street between which consists of shops and leads to a market place. On one side is the tomb and the other side has the mosque and madrasa. The style of the monument represents the Islamic architecture of Cairo.

The three reached the mosque. A police car came along with them. The Indian diplomat joined them as well. After glancing at buildings on both sides of the road, he went inside the right – the mosque. The police sealed the buildings and stopped the visitors. Everyone started searching for the barrel. Neel was looking carefully at each and every corner of the building. Jay went into the left building. He showed the police the photographs of the barrel.

After a while, Neel came out of the building as he had discovered nothing. He started moving towards the left building. He stopped for a while and glanced at the roof of the buildings. He found nothing. As he lowered his eyes to see the entrance of the building, his eyes paused at a point.

A wooden rod was attached to the entrance of the building. It was high enough not to be noticed. Lamps were hung on the rod and suspended till the entrance, so that the light would directly fall on the entrance. In between the lamps, a string was attached from which the barrel was suspended.

A smile appeared on Neel's face. They had found the second artefact in Cairo. After pausing for a while, he shouted, 'Found it!'

Jay and Avantika came towards Neel and saw the barrel. Both of them smiled and hugged each other. The police untied the string and brought the barrel down. Neel took it in his hand. His eyes were eagerly waiting to see the barrel.

The police took the barrel and left. Neel, Jay and Avantika went back to the safe house. Neel updated Raghu about the discovery. He congratulated him and wished him all the best for the next hunt.

'So, Mr James Bond, we have discovered two artefacts. Do you wish to explore Cairo? See the pyramids?' said Jay when Neel finished his call.

'Well Raghu will call me in an hour. And then we will know the flight timings. If we get time tomorrow, we will go to see the pyramids,' said Neel.

'So it's time for me to ask Raghu to extend the Cairo trip,' said Jay.

'Oh! You think you can do that?' teased Neel.

'Of course! He won't let me down,' said Jay.

'Then show us your magic! You can call him. Or shall I dial the number?'

'No, I will call him. But not now! First, let me see what time the flight is. If it is tomorrow or day after tomorrow, then it is fine. Why should I waste my talent?'

'You think you are talented?' asked Neel.

'That's why I'm with you,' said Jay smiling.

Neel paused for a while and said, 'Ya, that's right!'

'Hurry up Avantika. It is ten,' said Neel as he entered the house. The Indian diplomat had arranged a visit to the pyramids. Yes, the flight was after a day. The artefact had been found and they had a day to explore Giza.

Avantika came out of her room and said, 'It's not me, Jay is late.'

Neel shouted out his name and in no time, he came out of his room.

'I am on time!' said Jay.

They moved out of the house and headed towards their destination, The Great Pyramids of Giza. One of the seven wonders of the world. The oldest wonder of the world. The non-destroyed and the biggest wonder of the world.

The three reached the pyramids. They were amazed to say the least. A huge structure still standing and in perfect shape. Besides the pyramids was the Great Sphinx.

They went close to the pyramids, clicked photos and took it all in. It was awe-inspiring. The big brown blocks lay one on top of another and the perfect shape amazed them.

They enjoyed walking around the pyramids and headed back to the safe house. They had to catch a flight at midnight.

'And the next destination is?' asked Avantika when they reached the house.

'Cape Town!' said Neel.

Cape Town, South Africa

The southernmost point of Africa is filled with nature's beauty. The sunrise and sunset at the point is extraordinary. The large mountains, the greenery and the blue sea are the essence of South Africa.

The three reached Cape Town after a long journey of twenty hours. The city was bathed in warm bright sunlight. It was afternoon time and the temperature was high. They started to feel the heat as they landed. The Indian diplomat was waiting for them at the airport.

'Welcome to Cape Town sir,' said the diplomat.

'Thank you for receiving us,' said Neel.

They went directly to a hotel. The Government of India had planned their stay at the hotel. They knew the places they wanted to search – the Diaz Cross, aka Da Gama Cross. Neel told the Indian diplomat about the place.

'When do we go? Right now or tomorrow?' asked the diplomat.

'We need to search the place as soon as possible. We need to inform the police so that they can accompany us,' said Neel.

'I have informed the police. They will be with us when we are ready to go. We need to decide the time.'

Neel glanced at his phone. He opened the clock in it. It showed 2:00 p.m. He paused for a second and said, 'I think we should go right now! How much time do we need to get there?'

'An hour and a half.'

'Let's move then!'

The diplomat called the police and informed them about the visit.

'Which artefact is placed hidden in the Cape of Good Hope?' asked the diplomat.

'It's not at the Cape of Good Hope. It's at the Da Gama Cross near it. We think a bell is hidden there,' said Neel.

'Fine, the police will be here in a while. We should get going,' said the diplomat.

They headed towards their destination followed by a police car. They enjoyed the drive as they covered much of Cape Town en route. It was as beautiful as its name.

Da Gama Cross had been erected in remembrance of Vasco da Gama. He had landed in Cape Town at that place. A white monument with a cross on its head stands on an open ground with sea on one side. The greenery of the area with the blue sea behind is breathtaking. The name 'Da Gama' is carved on the monument along with the year 1497 – the year when Vasco da Gama had visited the Cape of Good Hope.

As soon as Neel glanced at the monument, he saw the bell hung up on the cross. The bell was attached in such a way that no one would ever know that the bell didn't belong there. Neel showed the bell to Avantika. The police then managed to remove the bell. The year '1498' was carved on the bell. It was the year when Vasco da Gama had reached India after his first voyage.

Neel had made his third discovery. The third artefact had not been difficult to find. He saw the bell and handed it to the police. The bell would be sent back to Oman where it had been retrieved in the first place.

They went back to the hotel. Neel informed Raghu about the third artefact. So now, their next destination was Mozambique, which was right next to South Africa.

'The next place is Maputo in Mozambique. When do we leave?' asked Jay.

The Indian diplomat said, 'We will arrange your departure. You can leave tomorrow itself.'

'Fine! And thank you for your time,' said Neel.

The sun had set and the three were tired. After having dinner, they retired to bed. Avantika was right next to Neel. He gave her a goodnight kiss and they fell into a long and deep sleep.

Neel's phone vibrated in the middle of the night. That disturbed his sleep. He opened his eyes with effort. A notification about a message blinked. He unlocked the phone and saw the message. It was from the Indian diplomat. He had arranged a special plane for them to get to Maputo. Neel thanked him.

He got up from his bed and had glass of water. He went near the window and glanced at the road. The road was empty. Suddenly, he felt someone behind him. He turned around and saw Avantika. She hugged him tightly and said softly, 'Why are you here, dear?'

'Nothing, it was the diplomat. He said he arranged a plane for us to get to Maputo tomorrow at 11 a.m.'

'So nice of the Indian people working here! It feels like home,' said Avantika.

'Yes, it's really appreciable. Now let's go to bed. I want to sleep.'

'Alone? I too am sleepy. You disturbed my sleep and now you are giving it back to me! Make me sleep!' she said and moved towards the bed.

Neel and Avantika slept in each other's arms. Her head lay on Neel's shoulder with one hand on his chest. He put both his hands around her body.

'It feels like heaven. I want every night to pass this way,' Avantika said and kissed Neel. He kissed her back. Their passionate love made the night even more wonderful.

The next morning, after getting ready, they headed towards the airport. The diplomat said the Indian Embassy in Maputo would help them there.

The plane took off and they reached Maputo in another two-and-a-half hours.

Maputo, Mozambique

The Indian diplomat in Maputo received them at the Maputo airport. They moved towards the safe house in Maputo. The biggest city in Mozambique, Maputo is its capital. It is situated along the coast. The city has expanded in all the directions and there is a healthy mix of lush vegetation and modern construction.

'There are two places in Maputo that we have to visit,' said Neel to the Indian diplomat when they reached the safe house.

'Please let me know which ones, so I can arrange things accordingly,' said the diplomat.

'The Portuguese school of Mozambique and Ilha dos Portuguese – the island,' said Neel.

'You want to visit them just because their names have 'Portuguese' in it?' asked Avantika.

'What other option do we have? There is nothing in Maputo named after Vasco da Gama. The map points to the artefact being hidden in Maputo. And it is a cannon ball, I think,' said Jay.

'Yes, it is a cannon ball but the mark made on the map is slightly above Maputo. It is along the coast, but I don't think it is exactly in Maputo,' said Neel.

'Which other place do we have in Mozambique?' asked Avantika.

'I don't know! But do one thing. Find monuments of Vasco da Gama in Mozambique. The map doesn't have any names on it. Not even of the places or the cities or countries. We must find the places of the monuments,' said Neel.

Jay searched it on the internet and said, 'There is a monument of Vasco da Gama on the Island of Mozambique which is far away from here. It is at the other end of Mozambique.'

'I don't think it can be there. Search again,' said Neel.

'There is another monument in Inhambane. I am tracing its location,' said Avantika after a while.

'Yes, I know about it. It is about five hundred kilometres from Maputo,' said the diplomat.

'Is it near the coast?' asked Neel.

'Yes!' said Avantika.

'The fourth artefact is at Inhambane then,' concluded Neel.

'We can go there tomorrow,' said the diplomat.

'Fine, we leave tomorrow! Meanwhile, can you tell the police to check the school and the island?' said Neel.

'Sure,' said the diplomat and left.

It was evening time. The three rested on the couch in the living area of the house.

'The city is beautiful! It gives me the feeling of being in Mumbai,' said Avantika.

'Yes, maybe because of the coastline,' said Neel.

'I hope we find the next artefact tomorrow,' said Jay.

'We will!' said Avantika.

'I think we should have dinner,' interrupted Neel.

'I like that idea the most. Let me order something,' said Jay.

'Well, let's go out for dinner and explore some of Mozambique,' said Neel.

'Are you serious?' asked Avantika.

'Yes, of course,' said Neel.

'The diplomat told me that he has arranged a car for us to get to Inhambane tomorrow,' said Jay with his eyes on the phone.

'A car? Isn't he coming with us?' asked Neel.

'Yes, he is,' said Jay.

'How much time will it take to get there?' asked Neel.

'About six hours,' said Jay.

'It's a long journey!' said Neel.

'Then get ready and go have dinner,' said Jay.

'Yes, boss!' said Neel and laughed.

Jay and Avantika laughed as well. A car and a driver were already waiting outside the house. They went to a hotel which Jay had chosen, and tried various dishes. Language was a big problem but the driver helped them with the translation. The driver knew English and that was a big relief for them.

They enjoyed the dinner. Jay paid the bill and they started moving towards the car. Avantika stopped Neel from entering the car.

'I think the hotel is close by. We could walk,' said Avantika.

'What? Are you sure? You don't know the road to the house,' said Jay.

'You could help. Go to the house and send me the location. Simple!' said Avantika.

'But Avantika, it's late! We have a busy day tomorrow,' said Neel.

'You don't want to take a walk with me?' asked Avantika, looking into Neel's eyes.

'Yes, I do, but...' said Neel and paused.

'No problem, I will go and send you the location. And if you need the car, just call me and I will send the car wherever you are,' said Jay.

'Yes, no problem,' said Avantika.

Avantika asked the driver where the sea was. The shore was nearby. Jay and the driver went back to the house. Neel and Avantika went to the sea shore for a wonderful walk.

'We are in an unknown city. We don't know the place. It is not safe to walk at this time,' said Neel.

'What fear do I have when you are with me? And that's the adventure Neel! Going for a walk at an unknown place. No one knows us here and we don't know anyone either. Isn't it thrilling?' said Avantika. She held Neel by his hand. She landed her head on his shoulder and walked around the shore.

Night had fallen. The sea was calm. The sea waves were touching their feet. The cold breeze hit their bodies.

'I am very happy Neel. It is amazing to have you in my life,' said Avantika.

'Yes, miss. You are my strength. I could never imagine doing this all alone. This wonderful and adventurous trip has not only given me my wife back, but it has also raised my capabilities. It has given me more strength and more wisdom. This trip is the most wonderful trip of my life and always will be,' said Neel.

'Yes, I was about to tell you the same thing. I want to tell you something,' said Avantika. They stopped walking and faced each other.

'What? Feel free to tell me anything.'

'I want to tell you that, this trip has been amazing! Let's make it more amazing! I don't know how to tell you...' said Avantika.

'What I am trying to say is that I think we should think about having a child.'

'A kid! You mean…'

'Yes! Isn't it the right time?'

'Yes, but let's just wait till we complete the mission.'

'Yes, maybe you are right!'

'Avantika,' said Neel and kept his hands on her shoulders. 'I have an idea! There have been a lot of problems in our marriage. But we survived. That's the power of our love. I think, after this mission, we should marry once again or just have a reception to celebrate our marriage. What do you think?'

'Yes, that's a wonderful idea. A new start!'

'Fine, then we will plan this mission,' said Neel and hugged her.

'It's so warm in here!' said Avantika when she hugged him back.

Neel smiled and so did Avantika. She closed her eyes and felt the warmth. After a while, she dialled Jay's number and told him to send the car to pick them up. They slept well that night in each other's arms.

The next day, they left for Inhambane. A police car accompanied them. The journey was long. They had to cross most of Mozambique to get to Inhambane. The road was largely along the coastline. They had lunch midway and the diplomat made them taste the special dishes of Mozambique.

'How do you feel here in Mozambique? Away from our country?' Jay asked the diplomat.

'We serve our nation and that's the biggest thing for me,' replied the diplomat. 'And it's not very different from India. We miss working in India but every place is the same when we work for our nation.'

'That's great,' said Neel and they chatted as the car made its way to their destination.

After the long journey, the police took them straight to the monument. The statue of Vasco da Gama is erected in the city and is not frequented by tourists.

Neel scanned the monument and found nothing. He had to find the cannon ball. He went around the monument in vain.

'The soil is loose! We should dig the place and check,' said Avantika pointing to the ground.

The police made arrangements to dig the place. After a while, they found something hard. Neel was sure it was cannon ball. After digging the surrounding soil, the cannon ball was clearly visible.

The cannon ball had a 'VS' mark on it. Neel gave it to the police.

'What does the mark stands for? VS?' asked Neel.

'I think they are the initials of Vicente Sodre! He was the uncle of Vasco da Gama. The ship found in Oman belonged to him,' said Jay.

'That's great! We found it,' said Neel.

'The shipwreck in Oman was first discovered in May 1998. More than two thousand artefacts were recovered in the shipwreck. The ship *Esmeralda* belonged to Vicente Sodre and Bras Sodre,' said Jay.

In the evening, they returned to Maputo with the cannon ball. The embassy in Maputo arranged for their departure. The next destination was Mombasa in Kenya.

They had their flight the next day. They reached the hotel late at night. They were tired and they retired to bed as soon as they reached. They had their dinner on the way. The diplomat told them that he would drop them at the airport the next day.

The next day, the diplomat reached the hotel in the morning. The three were ready for their next destination.

'I have made your arrangements in Mombasa. The people from the embassy in Mombasa will be there at the airport to receive you,' said the diplomat as they headed to the airport.

'Yes, thank you for your time and help. We really appreciate your help,' said Neel.

'You are always welcome,' said the diplomat as the car stopped at the entrance of the airport.

Mombasa, Kenya

The city in Kenya is located near the coast. Vasco da Gama landed in Mombasa on 7 April 1498.

'Vasco da Gama hotel is in Mombasa, named after Vasco da Gama,' said Avantika when they reached the Moi International Airport. The diplomat was waiting to receive them there.

'We can tell the police to check the hotel and the CCTV footage. What more do we have?' said Neel.

'Fort Jesus Museum. It was built by the Portuguese in 1593. Omani people captured the fort in 1698. I think the beads may be hidden there,' said Avantika.

'Okay, let's go,' said Neel.

The Indian diplomat in Mombasa arranged the visit to the fort. He first took them to the hotel, where their accommodation was arranged.

'We need to check the Fort Jesus. We need the police with us,' said Neel to the diplomat.

The diplomat had already arranged everything. Soon after, they left for Fort Jesus. The fort, which had been converted into a museum, is located near the coast. Many articles stored at the fort belong to the Portuguese.

'Can you show me the photos of the beads?' said the diplomat.

Neel took out the photographs of the beads from his bag. He showed it to the diplomat. The beads were the three piece structures made of stone or copper. They were round or oval in shape and were used as decorations.

'Do they have CCTV cameras at the fort?' asked Neel.

'Yes, but only a couple,' said the diplomat.

They reached the fort and entered the museum. The museum had ornaments, jewellery and many other precious things displayed in cases. Neel scanned each and every thing as fast as possible.

He heard Avantika calling him on the other side of the museum. He went there and saw the place.

'Mombasa Wreck Excavation,' read out Neel.

The section had artefacts which had been found during the excavation in Mombasa. Among the all artefacts, the missing beads had been carefully laid. No one would notice them. The beads had white and purple coloured stripes on it. He took them in his hand. Found!

He took them to the police and handed the fifth artefact to them. After carefully placing the artefacts in safe hands, they returned to the hotel.

'Where is the next place in Kenya?' asked the diplomat.

'Malindi,' said Neel.

'It is a hundred and twenty kilometres from Mombasa. We can go there tomorrow,' said the diplomat. 'Which artefact is hidden in Malindi?'

'It's a sheave!'

'I think there is a monument in Malindi which is erected in memory of Vasco da Gama? Right?' Neel asked.

'Yes, we need to get there tomorrow. We will find the sixth artefact there.'

After the discussion, the diplomat left. They planned their visit to Malindi the next day. Neel, Avantika and Jay had dinner early and sat in the living room.

'I am happy we found the artefacts without much trouble,' said Neel.

'Yes, you helped a lot!' said Avantika.

'Thank you! It was my job,' replied Neel.

'We have three more to find, out of which two are in India,' said Avantika.

'One is in Calicut. I think that will not be difficult to find,' said Neel.

'And the other is in Madayi. We have no idea about Madayi though,' said Avantika.

'Don't worry Avantika! We've found five of them. Did we have any idea about them before we did? We will find the ones in India too,' said Neel smiling.

'Sure,' said Avantika.

'Let's sleep now. We need to get to Malindi early tomorrow,' said Jay and yawned.

'Let's go wife!' said Neel looking right into Avantika's eyes.

Malindi, Kenya

'Vasco da Gama came to Malindi twice – on 13 April 1498 and on 14 January 1499,' said Neel when they reached the Vasco da Gama pillar in Malindi.

'The first time when he was heading to India, and the next time when he was returning from India,' said Avantika.

'Where is the artefact then? The pillar is right in front of me. But there's nothing here,' said Jay.

'The map shows the sheave is here. It has to be here!' said Neel.

The Vasco da Gama pillar in Malindi is a white monument with a cross on top. It is located away from the city near the coast. The rocks along the coast and the water trapped by them forms a pool. The sea-facing monument is splashed with the waves from time to time.

'The best option is to dig the area,' said Jay.

'But we are not sure Jay,' said Neel.

'We have no other option,' said Jay.

'Fine, then let's try that' said Neel.

Neel told the diplomat to arrange some people to dig around the monument. The police were already with them. They started digging around the monument. After a while, they found the sheave behind the monument.

The sheave is a circular object used like a pulley for lifting. It also functions like a handle. Neel took the copper-alloy sheave in his hand.

'May be this was used for heavy loads,' he said.

'We finally found it,' said Jay in glee.

Taking the sixth artefact with them, they returned to Mombasa. They went to their hotel, while the police took the artefact with them.

The night fell. Neel called Raghu and updated him about the sixth discovery.

'That's great. I have booked your flight back to Bengaluru tomorrow. Then we will hunt for the remaining two artefacts,' said Raghu.

'Yes, sir. I am waiting to get back to India. It's been so long,' said Neel.

'I will be there to receive you tomorrow. I have also arranged for the return of the artefacts to Oman. They will be returned as soon as possible.'

'Fine, sir. See you tomorrow,' said Neel.

Neel had completed his mission overseas successfully. He was now waiting to get back home. He was feeling relaxed.

'I can't wait to go back to India,' said Neel to Avantika. She was standing right next to him in the balcony of the hotel. They had finished their dinner and were relaxing. They were ready for their flight back home.

'Finally, this long trip gave me my love back,' said Avantika.

'Yes, and it gave me you! I love you my dear wife! I think we should celebrate after this mission,' said Neel.

'We will celebrate. I don't want to get away from you now,' she said, and raised herself on her toes and kissed him on his cheek.

'I love my job when you are by my side. I want you on every mission,' said Neel and hugged her tightly.

The stars were beautiful in the sky. The night was dark and the moon was glowing in the darkness. The cold breeze of the dark night touched their bodies. But they kept themselves warm by not letting go of each other. They kissed passionately and enjoyed the last leg of their foreign trip.

They retired to bed and slept in peace. The next day, Jay woke them up early in the morning.

'What is it Jay?' said Neel rubbing his eyes, as he opened the door.

'Get ready! We have to go!' said Jay.

'It is just seven. We have the flight at ten!' said Neel.

'We can't be late, Neel.'

'You wait then! We will get ready by eight and then leave for the airport.'

'I'm waiting. Get ready fast.'

They left for the airport at eight. The plane took off at ten. They had to wait twelve long hours to reach Bengaluru. They reached the Kempegowda International Airport in Bengaluru at 7:30 in the evening.

Bengaluru, India

They reached the airport and Raghu was at the airport to receive them.

'Welcome back, Neel!' said Raghu and hugged Neel.

'Thanks sir! I am glad you came to the airport,' said Neel.

Raghu saw Avantika and said, 'I am happy for both of you.'

Avantika smiled and so did everyone else. Jay felt a sense of relief when he met Raghu. They went towards the government quarters.

They had their dinner together and discussed the two artefacts in India and also about the six that they had recovered.

'The next place is Madayi,' said Neel when Raghu asked about the further plan of action.

'We will leave early in the morning for Madayi,' said Raghu.

As planned, they stayed the night there and left for Madayi early in the morning. Raghu joined them in the next artefact hunt. Madayi is about three hundred and forty kilometres from Bengaluru. The local police team joined them in Madayi.

Madayi is a small village in Kerala located on the coast of the Arabian Sea. The Pilgrim Ship incident took place in Madayi.

'So what have we got Neel? Which place do we visit in Madayi?' asked Raghu.

'Sir, I think it is in a mosque. The Madayi Palli mosque in Pazhayangadi,' said Neel.

'And what's special about it?' asked Raghu.

'Sir, the marble used for the construction of the Mosque is said to have been brought from Mecca. The ship that Vasco da Gama captured was heading for Mecca. So, I think the coin is in the mosque,' said Neel.

'Fine, let's check then,' said Raghu.

They reached the mosque. It was located away from Madayi and is one of the oldest mosques in madayi. They went into the mosque and scanned the place attentively.

Jay was the one to find it this time. The topmost portion of the middle column of the mosque had the coin stuck on it. The old historic Cruzado coin, the Portuguese coin had lost its colour after lying in the sea for hundreds of years. But the Portuguese seal was clearly visible on it.

They removed the coin from the column and took it with them. The seventh artefact had been found and they were now one short from completing the mission.

'Now the last coin in Calicut and the mission is over!' said Jay.

'Fine! You proceed to Calicut and I will meet you in Chennai,' said Raghu.

'Sir, it will be great if you join us in finding the last artefact,' said Neel.

'Yes, but I have some urgent business to take care of. You carry on with the hunt and return successful,' said Raghu.

The three proceeded towards Calicut without Raghu. Calicut or Kozhikode is about a hundred and twenty kilometres from Madayi. It is located southwards and is near the Arabian Sea. Close to the Calicut city is a small village called Kappad. It is the place where Vasco da Gama first landed in India. A monument in Kappad has been erected to commemorate the event. It is a historical place. The place where the first Portuguese sailor stepped foot in India. Vasco da Gama was successful in his mission to find the first sea route to India.

Kozhikode (Calicut), India

Neel, Avantika and Jay reached Kozhikode in the evening. They decided to visit Kappad the next day. They went directly to a hotel. Kappad is eighteen kilometres from Kozhikode. The local police had arranged their trip for the next day.

'This is the last night of our mission. We will be free tomorrow,' said Neel to Avantika.

'Yes, I can't wait to go home,' said Avantika.

'So what have you planned? After the mission?'

'Nothing! Just go home and rest with you by my side.'

Neel hugged her. 'Hey, what about a walk? On the beach? Only you and me?' said Avantika.

'Not a bad idea,' said Neel.

'Let's go!' said Avantika. They took the police car and headed towards the beach. The car had neither a radio nor a music player.

'The police life is so boring! There is no music in a policeman's life,' said Avantika.

'As long as you are with me, I have music in my life,' said Neel and smiled. Avantika smiled back.

They reached the beach. It was dark. They parked the car and went to the shore. The cold breeze energised Neel.

'It's so calm here! After all, a walk on the beach in our own country is the best of all,' said Avantika.

'You said it right. C'mon now, let's go,' said Neel. He held her hand and went close to the water. The water made their feet wet. The waves touched their feet and retreated, taking some sand with them.

'Wow, it's amazing! It feels like the land beneath my feet is getting away,' said Avantika and laughed.

Neel smiled and watched her enjoy herself. She was laughing and enjoying the water. Her laughter made him smile. Her laughter made him love her again. He pulled her towards him and hugged her tightly. It made their noses touch each other's. They sensed each other's breath. They touched each other's faces. And then they kissed passionately.

They went for a long walk on the beach.

'At last, the mission will be over tomorrow. I feel at peace,' said Avantika.

'Tell me what to do when this will be over?'

'Rest!' said Avantika with a deep sigh.

'I mean after that,' Neel smiled.

'Then celebrate.'

'Fine, we will plan it well!'

●

The next day, they reached the Vasco da Gama memorial on Kappad beach.

'Vasco da Gama landed here in the year 1498,' Avantika read out the words carved on the monument.

'The coin is right beneath the marble plate!' said Avantika spotting the coin. The coin was placed beneath the plate on which the words were carved. Jay removed the coin. It was a gold coin with the Portuguese seal on it.

'We found it!' said Jay.

'Mission complete!' said Neel.

With the coin, they went back to Kozhikode. After a while, Neel called Raghu and informed him about the coin. Raghu told them to head to the Calicut airport. A special flight for them had been arranged from Calicut to Chennai.

They reached the hotel in Kozhikode, packed their things and headed out of the hotel. Jay was at the counter of the hotel, taking care of the formalities. Neel and Avantika were waiting for him in the car. He came out of the hotel and sat in the car.

'Finally. We have done it Neel. Say thanks to me,' said Jay.

'Thanks Jay!' said Neel.

'Thank you very much Jay!' said Avantika.

'Thank you, both of you. Let's leave now,' said Jay. The car took them to the airport and the plane finally took them back to Chennai.

They reached Chennai after the ninety-minute journey.

Chennai, India

They handed the artefact to the police department and headed back to their home. This time, Avantika went with Neel. They no longer had to live separate lives.

'Home, sweet home!' said Avantika when they reached home.

'Home sweet home with you,' said Neel and hugged Avantika. 'Last time I left, I was alone, and now I have you.'

'Last time I left, I was wrong. This time I am right,' she said and planted a kiss on his forehead.

The night was extraordinary and so was their love. They slept little and chatted more. They spoke less and connected more. The words were few, but the sensations more. The eyes were shut and they saw each other's souls. The differences were less and togetherness was more. The night was dark and the love was bright. The moon and the stars glowed and so did their souls.

The next morning, Neel got up late. He checked his phone. He had a missed call from Jay and Raghu each. He called Raghu first.

'Neel, I want you in my office as soon as possible. I have a serious matter to discuss,' said Raghu.

Neel said, 'Fine sir, I will be there.' Then he called Jay.

'I don't know what's the matter. Raghu has called us both to his office,' said Jay over the phone.

Neel and Jay went to the office. They entered Raghu's cabin.

'Have a seat. I have a serious matter to discuss,' said Raghu.

'What is wrong sir?' asked Neel.

'Yesterday, we found Akash Gupta. He is alive!'

'What? How is that possible? I saw his hanging body with my own eyes,' said Neel, shocked. It was a huge surprise for Neel and Jay.

'Yes, the body was not his! It was a look-alike body with plastic surgery done on the face,' said Raghu.

'What the hell!'

'You can go and check! And see the truth for yourself,' said Raghu and they headed towards the place where Akash was kept.

Neel entered the room alone. Akash was tied to the chair. Neel sat on a chair in front of him. Akash smiled when he saw Neel. Neel was in shock and that made Akash smile.

'Why are you smiling? Do you think it's funny to waste the time of the police?' asked Neel.

'Everything is a joke Neel. You are a joke! You are a fool!' said Akash in anger.

'I want to know the truth. You are dead already. I will never hesitate to kill you for real and I will never get caught.'

Akash laughed loudly. 'You think you can kill me?'

'Shut up and answer my question.'

'Neel, you can't do anything! You are hopeless and helpless. Nothing is in your reach now.'

'Now means?'

'Let's start from the beginning! It will be fun.'

'Go ahead.'

'I killed myself and you believed it. You didn't even test the body! You handed the body to my family and everyone thought I was dead!'

'And why did you do that?'

'Have patience Neel! I am sure when you leave this place, you will have your eyes wet with tears.'

'Go on. Continue.'

'The body was masked with my face by plastic surgery. Only Shivam knew that I was not dead. Shankar was a mad fellow and I lost my dear friend Shivam. Shivam and I had planned my fake suicide. I got popularity. I became famous like never before. Shivam managed the theft of the artefacts with Shankar and kept them in the places where you would find them. Meanwhile, after my suicide, you had to leave for Oman and my suicide case was closed. The case of the missing artefacts closed my suicide case. And I became free!'

'And why did you steal the artefacts?'

'For history, my dear friend! You are now well informed about the Pilgrim Ship incident. That part of history needs light! And that was only possible after the artefact robbery.'

'But we found the artefacts and no one knows about them.'

'Oh really? You think that? Then I will shock you once more.'

'What are you talking about?'

'Neel, I make films! I can show anything. I can also arrange everything. I can change anything and I can make anything popular. People need money Neel! And I need popularity. I need to make history!'

'Get to the point.'

'People in your department are not trustworthy, Neel. Be careful of them. They can do anything for money. At least in India, anyone can compromise with his or her duty for money!'

'But not officers like me!'

'Yes, of course! You are a good officer. But when I can't manage people like you, then I make them work for me indirectly! Like you did! You found the artefacts for me.'

'The artefacts are with the police and many of them have reached Oman.'

'Yes, that's true, and I don't need the artefacts.'

'What is it then?'

'Because of my suicide, I got publicity. Because of the robbery, my case was closed. The artefacts were with me. I managed to hide them in eight different places. I had money and people needed money. Placing them at eight places was not an easy job. You know the Pilgrim Ship incident. I wanted to make a movie on Vasco da Gama. I had a technical team with me to hack every camera you went under during the artefact hunt. I made the clips. Wherever it wasn't possible to capture it in camera, I made people work for me. I recorded every single second. Your artefact hunt is recorded on camera. Starting from the first artefact till the eighth, I have recorded everything. The real hunt and the real robbery have been recorded. And I have it all! And I told you before, I am a director and I make films.'

Neel was shocked to hear him. 'But you can't release the film,' he said.

'Who said I can't? I have made the movie and I will release it. You can't stop it from being shown on YouTube, Facebook and many more social media websites. When people will know that I am not dead and I have made a film on a real robbery and a real artefact hunt, the websites will get flooded. It will be a super hit! And you can't kill me. I have already brought myself before the media yesterday. You can do nothing, Neel! Yes, I will go to jail. But that too just for a while. You don't have any proof to put me in jail for a long time.'

'You are absolutely mad!' said Neel and left fuming. He was completely shocked by Akash's words.

'Yes, I know. Thank you Neel. You are the hero in my movie. You are famous now! Be ready for the fame.'

Neel left the place. Without uttering a word, he left for home. The radio and the news channels were busy flashing the news about the movie and about Akash. Avantika was continuously calling Neel. Neel didn't answer any call. He reached home. Avantika opened the door and hugged him tightly.

'What is wrong with the world? Why are they playing with me? First I lost you and now I seem to have lost my credibility,' said Neel.

'Everything will be fine, my dear. Don't worry please.'

'I can't be a puppet. I was used. My skills were used!'

'No, Neel. You did your job and you found out the truth. That's all!'

Suddenly, the doorbell rang. Avantika opened the door. It was Jay.

'Don't worry Neel, I will handle it,' said Jay softly.

'I will resign! I can't stay here anymore! Are you coming with me, Avantika?' asked Neel.

'No, Neel. First talk to Raghu,' said Jay. 'I am calling him.'

Jay called Raghu and gave the phone to Neel. Neel told Raghu about submitting his resignation.

'Neel, you can go wherever you want, but I will not accept your resignation. The department needs you. The country needs you!' said Raghu.

'But sir. . .'

'Nothing! I will handle everything. You go for a holiday and don't worry about the situation,' interrupted Raghu.

Neel had no choice but to agree. He decided to go away from the city for a while.

'I will manage here. You both leave,' said Jay.

Neel and Avantika decided to leave Chennai as soon as possible.

'I hate holidays! We get into trouble during each one,' said Avantika when they relaxed in the train.

'I feel like never returning! By the way, will you now tell me where are we going? I followed you blindly like a small child!'

'We are going somewhere in the north. The place is a surprise.'

'But have you made the arrangements? Where do we stay?'

'I took all the money we had. We will stay in a village. Jay has his house there. It will not be a problem.'

'What? How did Jay get a house there?'

'He had once visited the place. He liked it and bought a small house there.'

'Fine and where is the place? At least describe it.'

'The mountains at the back, the river by the side, the beautiful blue sky and the green land. The birds and animals enjoying themselves. The silence of nature and we both alone in the silence.'

'Sounds so peaceful.'

'Yes, only you and me and nature!'

Neel put his hand around her neck. She rested her head on his hand and they closed their eyes. The train moved on and their hearts calmed down.

Epilogue

Somewhere in North India.

The sun was rising slowly. The yellow light was bathing the world. The darkness was vanishing. Neel and Avantika were sleeping. Suddenly Neel woke up with a jerk. He glanced at Avantika. She was sleeping. He planted a kiss on her cheeks and ran his fingers over her face. He got up from his bed and went towards the entrance of the house. Without making a sound, he opened the door. He glanced out and saw the open green ground in front of him. The cold breeze caressed his face and the sun rays made him squint.

'Good morning my dear husband,' Avantika said from behind.

'Good morning wife.'

'So what dream did you see? Why did you get up so suddenly?'

'I think, sometimes a jolt is good. It brings us to our senses. I had a good dream and that made me get up.'

'Will you tell me what it was about?'

'Yes, the dream was about us. We had a baby and the baby was crying. And that woke me up,' said Neel holding her hand in his.

'Oh! That's amazing! So you can look after the baby? That's good.'

'Yes, I can. I can look after you both, my twin soul.'

'Fine. Let's make something to eat,' said Avantika and started for the kitchen.

'Avantika, do you know what I am saying?' said Neel holding her hand.

'Yes, but it's not the right time. I need food to think.'

'Fine. I will make breakfast and you get ready!'

'Get ready for what?'

'We need to discuss about having the baby.'

'There is nothing to discuss.'

'So when will we have the baby?'

'It takes nine months,' said Avantika and laughed.

'So when do we begin?'

'I don't know.'

'Let us start today,' said Neel and looked deep into her eyes. She looked right back into his. They smiled and laughed. Suddenly, Avantika heard her phone ringing. It was Jay.

'Switch on the TV,' said Jay in an excited tone.

'Fine!' she said.

She ran and switched on the TV and tuned to a news channel. Neel stood beside her.

'The artefacts have been found! Akash Gupta arrested. The video he made leaked. It is on YouTube, Facebook and other networking sites. Despite the ban on the video, it has gone viral! Neel, you are a hero! Everyone is searching for you and your team,' Avantika read the news aloud.

'Why did the websites not remove the video?'

'They have removed, but still it is popular. I guess Akash has many people to put it on the websites from different accounts,' said Avantika.

'Fine, I have no problem now! No one can find me here,' said Neel.

'You have done nothing wrong. And people like you. Akash has made you popular! You are a hero among the people now. Everyone is looking for you,' said Avantika. 'So when do you make an entry? People are waiting to meet you.'

'At the right time!'